Discovering HER Heart

A BUENA HILLS ROMANCE

ALLISON GYGI

Published by Castlerod Press

Chicago, IL

Cover design by Raneé Clark of Sweetly Us Book Services

https://allisongygi.com

ISBN: 979-8-9860561-2-8

 Formatted with Vellum

For Anna

May you always love discovering new worlds through the pages of good books.

Chapter One

April

Nothing on earth could make a guy feel dumber than spending a Friday evening attempting to comprehend the inner workings of a calculus textbook. And Tyler Abernathy wasn't a dummy, no matter how much his grades sometimes said otherwise. Math just wasn't his subject. It never had been. If he didn't need the credits to fulfill his general education requirement in quantitative reasoning, he would've skipped retaking it altogether after failing his first semester.

He sat at the kitchen island in the home he shared with his cousin, Brad, grateful again that his journalism major didn't require any more math. His textbook lay open on the counter, though his attention was diverted to the Dodgers game streaming on the laptop right behind it. The Miami Marlins, his favorite team, were in town for a three-game series. What he'd give to be sitting in the stands rather than studying for his test next week.

But he'd already put off the torture by going to the game last night, promising he'd stay on task today. That promise was proving difficult to keep.

He glanced at his notes from his latest tutoring session sprawled out around the textbook like an explosion of leaflet paper. More like white flags of surrender. He picked up the nearest one and squinted at his tutor's chicken scratch, trying to decipher what it said. Giving up, he set it down and picked up another. This one was in his own writing, which wasn't much neater, but simpler to read. Too bad it wasn't any easier to understand.

Buzzing his lips, he scanned the kitchen, rubbing his temple with two fingers, trying to alleviate the oncoming stress headache. His eyes landed on the microwave. There was a large burn mark on the inside from the time Brad had tried to heat up a can of baked beans a few months after they'd moved in. He'd almost burned the house down with that mistake, making his dad question the wisdom of allowing his barely nineteen-year-old son and nephew to live in the house he'd inherited after his parents' deaths.

The five-bedroom bungalow had belonged to Brad's family for generations, since the founding of Buena Hills—a Los Angeles suburb not too far from USC's University Park campus. It had been a good home for the last four years. But with graduation looming in a little over a month, Tyler and Brad were heading off in different directions—a sports broadcasting internship in San Francisco for Brad and grad school at Berkeley for Tyler. Assuming he passed calculus.

He glared at his notes. *I better pass.*

And once his sisters and cousin moved in, things would look pretty different around the house. Uncle Brent was most likely happy about that.

"Pizza's here," Brad announced, barging through the swinging kitchen door. "I found these street rats outside. They looked hungry, so I invited them in for some food." He gestured to the four women filing in behind him.

Brad's sister, Bridget, known as Beej to everyone in the family except Grandma Abernathy, shoved her older brother as she passed him.

"Shut up, Brad. You're not as funny as you think you are. Besides, I paid for the pizzas. You all owe me seven bucks by the way." She wagged a finger at everyone else. Mumbles of agreement echoed through the room.

Tyler's sister, Elise, peered over his shoulder at the mess of notes on the counter. "Whatcha studying, big brother?"

He slid a piece of paper out of the way so she could see the book underneath. "I'll give you twenty bucks to disguise yourself as me and take my calculus test next week. You'd probably do better than me. Didn't you get an A when you took it in high school?"

"Heck no. I barely managed a B-minus. That dumb class killed my GPA." She scrunched her nose as she sat down next to him. "You could beg Hallie. She *did* get an A."

His sisters had always been much better students than he was. Somehow, the intelligence gene seemed to skip over him. He liked to think he was smart; he just hated school. Correction: he hated math. The rest of his classes weren't so bad.

He turned exaggerated puppy dog eyes on his youngest sister, who dropped onto the stool on his other side. Hallie laughed.

"You know you'd be able to internalize more of what you're learning if you turned off all the other distractions." She pointed to the laptop where the game was on commercial break.

Tyler rolled his eyes. His sister ... always the practical one. "I'm trying to minimize the agony."

"Well, someone's being dramatic." Beej's mouth curved up in amusement as she joined them at the island.

Before he could respond, Brad thumped the two pizzas down in front of them all, scattering the papers. He flipped open the top box and steam rose from the mountain of mozzarella, pepperoni, and olives. "Eat up while they're hot."

"Did you get Hawaiian?" Hallie asked.

Brad turned up his nose. "It's underneath. How you can eat that monstrosity is beyond me though. Pineapple on pizza is a crime to humanity."

"Says the guy who puts so much hot sauce on everything it over-powers whatever you're eating," Tyler said, gathering up the last of the papers and placing them in a haphazard pile in the center of the island. "I'm surprised you have any taste buds left."

Brad was too busy digging through the fridge for the hot sauce to respond, so Tyler turned his attention to the fourth woman in the room. Kendall was searching through the cabinets to the right of the stove, all three of them open.

"Plates are one door over," he said to her before pulling out a slice of Hawaiian from the box. A long string of cheese hung onto the rest of the pizza. Just the way he liked it. There could never be too much cheese.

She paused her search and faced the room. "How much time do I spend in this house? I know where the plates are."

"Then what are you doing?" With his pizza still in his hand, he walked over to her. Reaching into one of the open cabinets, he pulled out several plates and handed one to her.

Kendall accepted it with a shrug. "I'm getting a feel for the place. Trying to figure out what kind of kitchen supplies we'll have to work with once we move in."

"Hey, don't get ahead of yourself," Brad mumbled through a mouth full of pizza. He swallowed hard. "This place is still ours until July."

"It's never too soon to start planning. Three months will go by like that." She snapped her fingers.

"Speaking of the house," Beej said, filling a glass of water from the tap. "You two are the only ones living here since what's his name moved out."

What's his name's actual name was Christian. He hadn't lived in the house for over two years, longer than any of the girls had been living in Buena Hills, so it was weird that she was bringing him up now. He'd been one of Tyler's best friends since freshman year, so Brad had invited him to live with them when they'd moved into the house. They didn't see much of him anymore though. What was it about getting married that made a guy drop off the face of the planet?

Brad shot a suspicious look at his sister. "What're you getting at?"

"Well ..." Beej drew out the word longer than necessary. A sure sign she was up to something. She gestured to the other women. "We were talking the other day about those three extra bedrooms."

"What about them?" His eyes narrowed even more.

"What do you think about us moving in early?" she asked. "There are four of us, but any of us would be willing to share rooms."

"Absolutely not." Brad shook his head so hard that Tyler worried he'd give himself whiplash.

"Why not?" Hallie asked. "It could be one big family party. There's a reason we all go to this school, right?" Their family had a long-standing tradition of being proud Trojans, starting with Tyler's grandparents. "Well, I mean, I don't go here yet, but I will soon."

As an aspiring baker, she'd opted to take a year of culinary classes before starting her business degree at USC.

"Just because it's tradition, doesn't mean we all have to live in the same house." Brad's mouth twitched. "Besides, I'd hate for word to spread that I'm living with my little sister."

Beej stuck her tongue out at him. "You just don't want us to get in the way of your bachelor pad."

"It's not like you can throw parties here anyway," Kendall said, continuing the conversation. She joined them at the island, seemingly satisfied with her snooping. "You'd have the cops called on you in no time. The neighbors are already suspicious of two college-aged guys living in the neighborhood. Having us responsible family members here keeping you in line should help."

Kendall wasn't actually related to any of them, but she'd come to live with Tyler's family right before his senior year of high school, so she may as well be another one of his sisters. Though it had taken much of that year for her to finally acknowledge his existence. He didn't know what had spurred her trust issues with men. Elise knew, and he suspected his parents and Hallie did also, though none of them had ever elaborated on Kendall's past. And though he was curious, he valued his life too much to ask about it.

"Ty, would you help me out here?"

Brad's desperation brought Tyler back to the conversation. What were they talking about? Oh yeah, the house. "Actually, it might be nice to have more people splitting the utilities."

Brad threw his hands into the air. "Really, bruh? You're supposed to be on my side."

Truthfully, Tyler wasn't thrilled with the idea of sharing the house with the girls either. Not that he had any objection to them per se. His sisters were some of his favorite people in the world. But it was kind of nice not having to fight for time in the bathroom in the morning like he used to when he lived at home.

However, he did see the benefit to their plan. And it would only be for a few months. It might even allow him to cut down on his hours working at the university bookstore. That would free up more time for calculus. He glanced at his textbook and shuddered.

On second thought ...

"Anyway, we can talk about this later," Elise said with a wave of her hand, probably realizing, like Tyler, the pointless nature of the conversation. Having Brad and Beej living under the same roof wasn't the best idea. Their vastly different personalities made it difficult to get along, even if they did love each other. "Guess who I ran into on campus today?"

He paused, the slice of pizza halfway to his mouth. "Who?"

"Does Gemma Schalk ring a bell?"

"No way!" he shouted, much louder than he'd intended.

Hallie jumped a little, her slice of pizza dropping from her hand.

After sending an apologetic smile her way, he turned to Elise. "What's she doing in SoCal? She always insisted she'd go to college in Oregon."

Elise tore off a paper towel from the roll in the center of the island and wiped her hands. "She did, but she graduated last spring. She's starting her master's program down here in the fall and came early to help her grandma for the summer. Apparently, her grandpa died right before Christmas."

Tyler's stomach dropped. "He did? Poor Gem."

"Who's Gemma Schalk?" Beej asked, plucking an olive from Brad's pizza and popping it in her mouth.

Tyler helped himself to another slice of Hawaiian as he

explained. "She was my best friend when we lived in Santiago. Her mom taught at the same university as our dad." He'd thought about her a lot in the years since his family had moved away.

"Best friend, huh?" Brad nudged him with his elbow. "Or sweetheart?"

Tyler shook his head, a small laugh bubbling in his throat. "Nah, it wasn't like that. She was just one of the guys."

"She must not be hot, then." Brad winced when Kendall came up behind him and smacked the back of his scalp. "Oww! What was that for?"

"Why is it always about looks for you, Brad?" She reached over his shoulder and grabbed a slice of pepperoni from the box. Before taking a bite, she added, "It's no wonder you can't keep a girlfriend."

Brad slumped on his stool with a huff. "I'm doing perfectly fine in the lady department, thank you very much."

Tyler shared a doubtful look with his sisters. He couldn't even remember the last time Brad had been in a semi-serious relationship with anyone, let alone a serious one. Most of the women he'd dated didn't stick around for more than a few dates.

"Well, is she?" Brad asked, returning to his original statement.

Tyler didn't know how to answer that. The last time he'd seen Gemma, they were both awkward teenagers, covered in acne and braces and still growing into their bodies. He'd never really thought of her as pretty or not. She was just Gemma. His best friend. "I guess she was pretty."

"I invited her to go to the movie with us tonight," Elise said. "I hope that's okay."

"Are you kidding me?" He'd never heard a more pointless question than that. "Of course it's okay. I'd love to see her again. It's been way too long."

Seven years too long. She hadn't even come outside to say goodbye the morning his family left Santiago for good. And she wouldn't accept his calls in the weeks after either. Why was that? It couldn't have been because of what happened the night before.

Or could it?

Nah. He shook the thought away. There had to be something else that had caused her to ignore him.

"Great," Elise said. "I told her to meet us here at seven, so she should be here soon." Right on cue, a quiet knock came from the front door. She started to get up. "That's probably her."

Tyler stopped her with a hand on her arm. "I'll get it." He tried to keep the anticipation off his face so no one would catch how eager he was to see his childhood best friend.

But he *was* eager. Excited even. Speaking of her again had reminded him of how much he'd missed her.

He reached the entryway and all but threw the front door open. Then he froze. Standing in front of him was not the sixteen-year-old girl he'd left behind in Chile. Gone were the braces and frizzy pony-tail. Gone were the basketball shorts and baseball glove.

The woman in front of him was all feminine curves and loose, dark curls. Her smile, though uncertain, was no less familiar than he remembered. The light freckles still dotting her face gave her a more youthful look than her twenty-three years.

But even her freckles couldn't disguise what was staring him right in the face: Gemma Schalk was all grown-up.

Chapter Two

Thirteen Years Earlier

January

Sitting in the back seat of the rental van, Tyler tried really hard not to cry. Ten-year-old boys were supposed to be tough. But his eyes got all watery, so he blinked as fast as he could to make the tears go away.

Flicking the hood of his sweatshirt over his head, he refused to look out the window as Dad drove them through the streets of Santiago toward their new home for who knew how long.

This can't be happening, he thought, sliding down as low as he could go without falling off the seat. The safety belt cut into his stomach, but he ignored the pain and wiped the sweat from his forehead. It was way too hot to be January.

Instead of taking off the sweatshirt though, he pulled the strings to tighten the hood over his eyes. Maybe if he tried hard enough, he could pretend he was still in Miami and his family was on their way to the ocean for the day. He imagined their old SUV driving along the beach-lined road, palm trees swaying in the breeze. But when he finally looked out the window a minute later, what he saw was definitely *not* Miami. Walls lined the street instead of palm trees, protecting the houses behind them. The sand in his imagination was replaced by concrete, and a few stray dogs wandered around looking for scraps of food. It was as though he'd entered another world.

They left the main road and turned toward Lo-Barn-a-something. Mom had told him the name of where they'd be living a few days ago, but he hadn't been paying attention. And it wasn't home, so why should he learn it?

"Are we there yet?" Elise had asked the same thing every five minutes since they'd left the airport. Did she have to be so annoying? If she didn't stop leaning on him to look out his window, he was about to shove her back himself. He glared at her as Mom turned around in the front seat.

"Almost, sweetie," she said, smiling at Elise's excitement. "The GPS says we'll be there in three minutes."

"Is it a big house?" Hallie asked from the seat in front of Elise.

Dad made another turn. "Big enough for our family."

That's code for small. Oh great, Tyler would probably have to share a room with the girls. What a nightmare.

How could his parents do this? He would expect it from Mom— she tried to get Dad to move to random places all the time. A quaint cottage in the Cotswolds (what did quaint even mean anyway?). A fairy-tale village in Germany (Tyler hated fairy tales). The African savanna. The Amazon. Tokyo. Guam. And that wasn't even half the list.

But Dad? He'd always been able to talk her out of her stupid plans. Until now. Taking a research assignment in South America was all his horrible idea.

When he'd told the family about the assignment in Chile, Tyler had thought it was only a joke he was playing on Mom. Was there an equivalent to April Fools' Day in November? There should be.

But this was no November Fools. Not even a month after he'd told them the news, their house sold, and Tyler had to say goodbye to all his friends.

"Look at that!" Elise squealed. Her arm shot out to the side and barely missed hitting him right in the face.

He shoved it away.

"Ow! Mom, Tyler pushed me!"

He folded his arms in front of him. "Did not. Your arm was in my space."

Unfortunately for them all, Elise's yelling woke up Wes. He'd only been asleep for a few minutes after crying nonstop since the airport. His wails filled the car, sounding a lot more like a velociraptor than an almost two-year-old.

"Nice going, Tyler." Elise stuck her tongue out at him.

Mom turned around fast. Tyler had heard her use the expression "if looks could kill" before, but he never understood what that meant until now. "Come on, guys. Would you knock off the fighting?"

"She started it," he grumbled, slumping down in his seat again.

Elise glared at him. "Did not. I only wanted to see out the window. You always get the window seat."

"Enough." The way Mom said it stopped them both. "I don't care who started it. This fighting ends now."

She reached down to the floor behind her seat and picked up Wes's stuffed dog, then tossed it gently over his rear-facing car seat and into his lap. He grabbed it, snuggling it to his face. The crying finally stopped.

"And Ty," Mom said before turning back around, "we all know you're unhappy about being here, but please don't ruin the excitement for the rest of the family."

Tyler tapped his pointer finger to the side of his eye and flicked it forward in a salute. Whatever would get her to stop the nagging. Once she turned back around, he leaned over to Elise. "Tattletale," he hissed in her ear.

She stuck her tongue out, then gasped. "Is that our house?" And whoopee, she was back in his personal bubble.

He hadn't even noticed they'd stopped. He stared out the window at the solid white wall in front of them. It looked like the same material a lot of homes back in Florida were made from. Stucco, he thought he remembered Dad calling it. A solid, brown door stood in the middle of the wall.

Dad turned off the car and thumped his fingers on the steering wheel. "This is it. Home sweet home. What do you think?"

Tyler helped Elise unbuckle her seat belt. The sooner she left the car, the sooner she'd leave him alone. She launched over his lap and pressed her face against the window to look at the top of the house, the only part visible over the wall.

"I can't see very much," she said.

Mom chuckled. "You'll be able to see it better once we're in the yard. Come on. Everyone out. Let's go explore our new crib."

He rolled his eyes.

When Mom opened the back door to get Wes from his seat, Elise leaped over Tyler and jumped out of the car.

"Are you coming, Ty?" Mom asked, pulling Wes's hand away from the chunk of blonde hair he held in his tight little fist. She shook his arm, using her baby voice to talk to him.

Tyler was in no hurry to check out the *new crib*. "In a minute," he grumbled.

Mom sighed. He could practically feel her disappointment. "Look, honey, I understand this is hard for you."

"Do you, Mom?" He didn't try to hide his frustration. "I've heard you tell Dad how much you want to move. I just never thought you'd ever talk him into it."

Her sympathetic look made his stomach hurt. "Of course I understand. You had to leave your friends, your school, everything that's familiar to you. And now you're in this strange place with different customs, different smells, different foods ..."

Oh gosh. I didn't think about the food.

"But I know that if you give this place a chance, it won't be as bad as you're expecting it to be." She shrugged. "Who knows, you might find you like it here."

Yeah right.

"Just think about it." She squeezed his thigh, and he grunted, which only made her sigh again. "I won't ask you to be happy about this, but at least bring your moping inside the yard. Now that the car isn't running, the cool air will wear off fast. It'll get pretty hot in here."

It was already hot. His skin felt sticky with sweat. *I guess I can be miserable inside the stupid house.* He slid all the way out of his seat.

Then he climbed from the car and followed Mom through the gate, dragging his backpack on the ground behind him. When she went inside, he stayed where he was, finally getting his first look at the house.

Huh. It was different than their place in Miami. Maybe even a little bigger since there were three floors instead of two. It had straight walls and a mostly flat roof, which made Tyler picture a big box. Even the brown paint looked like cardboard. Not the prettiest house he'd ever seen, but it wasn't the tiny hut he was expecting from a Chilean house.

Still, it wasn't home.

He slung his backpack over one shoulder and grabbed the handles of his suitcases, which Dad had left right inside the gate. Then he walked up the path that led to the open front door, dragging his feet, even though Mom had told him a bunch of times to stop doing that since it scuffed up his shoes.

As he walked, he looked around the front yard. It wasn't huge, though a grassy patch seemed to lead to the backyard. He hoped there was a large enough area to play catch with Dad every day after he got home from work.

To the left of the grass, a wall made of the same thing as the one facing the street, except shorter, separated their house from the neighbors'. A girl's head peeked over the top of it, watching him. She was wearing a baseball cap, and two thick braids hung down both shoulders, dark frizzy curls spilling out of them. With her arms crossed on top of the wall, Tyler could barely see the baseball glove poking out from underneath them. She gave him a small smile, showing a little gap between her front teeth.

Curious, he left his suitcases on the pathway and went over to her. "Hi."

"Hi. My name's Gemma." She paused, looking him over. "Who are you?"

"Tyler."

She pulled herself onto the wall, swinging one leg over to

straddle it. Dirt streaked her basketball shorts. "Are you from America?"

He nodded, not sure what else to do. "Florida. I just moved here."

"I can see that." She kicked her sneaker against the wall over and over. "I'm from Oregon, but we've lived here for years. My mom teaches at one of the colleges here."

"Really? My dad will too." He coughed, trying not to sound too excited. He wasn't excited. Not even a little bit. "How old are you?"

"Ten," she said. "How old are you?"

"Ten." He pointed to the glove on the wall. "Do you play?"

"I can hold my own." She frowned. "If the boys would ever let me play with them."

Okay, maybe he was a little excited now. Gemma talked about other boys. Other boys who played baseball. *I wonder if they're any good.*

Back home, Tyler had spent all his free time on the baseball diamond. Being forced to quit his Little League team was the worst part of moving to this awful place. They'd barely missed out on the league championship title last season. Now he wouldn't have a chance to help them earn a second shot at the finals.

The possibility made him sad, so he tried not to think about it. "Why don't they let you play?" he asked Gemma instead.

She lifted her shoulders to her ears. "I'm a girl." She said it like it was obvious.

"That's stupid."

"Tell me about it." Resting her elbows on the wall, she leaned forward and put her chin on her hands. "But that's the way it's always been around here."

He still wasn't happy about being ripped away from everything he'd ever known, but if Gemma was as good as she said she was, he wouldn't mind playing with her when Dad was at work. "Do you want to play right now? I have my glove in my backpack."

"Sure!" She grabbed hers off the wall, then hopped down onto the grass next to him.

"Let me just bring my bags inside. I'll be right back." He turned toward his new house and found himself smiling for the first time since landing in Santiago. This still wasn't home, and he couldn't say he even liked being here. But maybe Mom was right. Living in a foreign country might not be as bad as he thought.

Chapter Three

"Hi, Tyler," Gemma squeaked. She cleared her throat. "Long time, no see, huh?"

It took all her effort to keep from slapping her forehead with the palm of her hand. Her full-ride academic scholarship and 4.0 GPA really paid off with that eloquent greeting. Pathetic.

Tyler stared back at her, his hand still gripping the doorknob. With his mouth hanging open a bit, he appeared to be in a state of shock at seeing her, of all people, standing on his front porch. Didn't Elise tell him she was coming?

"I ran into your sister on campus," she started to explain. "I thought she would've mentioned I was coming over tonight."

That seemed to snap him out of his trance. "She did." Then his face broke into a wide smile—the same signature Abernathy grin that all four kids had inherited from their father. "It's so good to see you."

Gemma's heart stuttered in response to his smile. *Knock it off,* she scolded the organ. *You're not a naïve kid anymore.*

By the looks of him, neither was he. Against her will, her eyes traveled down the front of him. The perfect amount of blond stubble lined his square jawline. Broad shoulders caused his black T-shirt to pull slightly across his chest, and she could only imagine the shape of his stomach underneath the fabric. Truth be told, she liked the mental picture.

Her eyes snapped back to his face, where they should've stayed all along. She was *not* just checking him out.

Before she knew what was happening, he stepped onto the porch and pulled her into a tight hug.

She froze, her arms pinned to her sides. What was this, a squeeze contest? She frowned as a zing of pleasure zipped through her at the feel of solid muscle pressed against her. Tyler Abernathy was no longer the scrawny sixteen-year-old kid she'd known in Santiago. There was some serious definition in those abs.

Focus. If she didn't reciprocate this hug, they might be forced to stand this way all night. And that would *not* be a good thing. Reluctantly, she wrapped her arms around his middle.

"I wish you'd have told me you were moving to California," Tyler said, stepping back. "You had to have known I'd be living down here."

"It slipped my mind, I guess," she said through an embarrassed chuckle.

That's my story, and I'm sticking to it. Failing to contact him had nothing to do with her desire to avoid him and the bad memories of their final night together. Nope, not at all.

Because Gemma *had* known there would be a strong likelihood of Tyler living in Southern California when she'd made the decision to move down here to help Gram. He had his sights set on following in his family's Trojan footsteps their entire friendship. But what were the odds of him ending up in the exact same suburb that Gram had lived in her entire married life?

Tyler shoved his fingers through his belt loops as he studied her, one side of his mouth lifting. Then he shook his head as his full smile broke through again. "Man, I can't believe it's been seven years, right?"

Gemma nodded slowly. She would've liked it to be more. Why had she even accepted Elise's invitation to hang out tonight? Spending Friday night in her sweats playing Rummikub with Gram and her quilting club sounded so much more appealing than fumbling through an entire evening with Tyler Abernathy.

Truth be told, there was a brief moment before she'd left the house when she'd considered wearing those same sweats here. Then she remembered that Cassie would have a conniption if she found out her sister had hung out with a guy—an attractive one at that—in what she'd dubbed her *comfort outfit*. They may be twins, but their similarities didn't extend to their clothing preferences. Cassie knew all the top fashion trends like the back of her hand, and Gemma—well, without her sister's help—would have no sense of fashion at all.

"What are we waiting out here for? Come on in. Are you hungry?" Tyler motioned her through the door and followed behind her, placing a light hand on the small of her back to guide her as she passed.

Her step faltered a bit at the unexpected contact, but she recovered quickly. A low rumble bubbled in her stomach, and she wasn't sure if it came because of the reminder that she hadn't eaten since lunch or because of his touch. Wasn't there some kind of rule book about physical affection between friends who hadn't seen each other for more than half a decade? If not, she should write one. Her fellow members of the Unrequited Love Club would eat it up. She'd win awards for sure. Maybe even a Pulitzer.

Except this wasn't love. It couldn't be. She hadn't seen the guy for seven years. Long enough to get over her silly crush on him. She didn't even know what kind of person he'd grown into. He could be a total jerk. *That's right, girl. Keep that thought firmly in your mind.* What she felt right now was strictly her body's reaction to human attraction. Because she could admit that Tyler had grown into a very handsome man. But that didn't mean a thing.

They passed through the swinging door into the kitchen. The conversation stopped and all focus landed on them. She rarely struggled with social anxiety, though the palpable curiosity of several of those in the room threatened to falsify that claim.

Hallie—wow, she looked different than the eleven-year-old she'd been the last time Gemma had seen her—hopped off her stool and skipped over to them, giving her a hug. "Hey! It's so good to see you. How are you?"

"I'm good. Thanks for letting me crash your party."

"Don't mention it," Hallie said. "Do you want some pizza before we go to the movie? We have extra."

Gemma breathed a shallow sigh of relief at the excuse to create some distance from Tyler. She stepped to the island as the stocky guy sitting next to Elise flipped open one of the boxes, revealing half a pepperoni pizza.

"I think there are a few slices of Hawaiian too," he said, handing her the last clean plate on the counter, "if you prefer that instead."

Gemma acknowledged him with an appreciative smile. "Pepperoni's fine. Thank you." She pulled off a slice and set it on the plate.

The guy held up the bottle at his elbow. "Hot sauce?"

She couldn't help a little chuckle. "I'm good, thanks." *Who puts hot sauce on pizza?* She turned back to Hallie. "All you need is Wes here and you'd have the whole family in Southern California."

"He's in ninth this year," Hallie responded. "Just wait a few years and it could happen. Unless Elise carries out her plan of becoming a world traveler before then."

"Little Wes is in high school now?" Gemma asked. The youngest Abernathy was only eight when the family moved away from Chile. "I can't believe it."

"I tell him that frequently."

She startled at Tyler's voice right behind her. When had he left the doorway? He winked at her when she looked at him, his mouth lifting into a mischievous smirk.

Her bottom lip caught between her teeth. How did he still have that frustrating ability to make her smile—even when she didn't want to—after all this time? It was so unfair.

"Does this coffee maker belong to either of you?" All heads turned to the only other brunette in the room besides Gemma. She held up the empty appliance. "Or will it be staying with the house?"

"This isn't your place!" This came from the guy sitting next to Elise. Gemma wished she'd gotten his name. He marched over to the unknown woman. Yanking the carafe from her hand, he placed it back on the counter.

"Not yet," she said, obviously not intimidated by the guy's hostility.

Whatever was going on between the two of them, Gemma silently thanked them. Their little feud turned the attention away from her for the moment.

But not long enough. Only a second later, Tyler's hand on her shoulder killed her amusement. Why was he touching her again? Was he this physical with everyone? She didn't remember this about him when they were teenagers.

"Hey, Slugger," he said. "Let me introduce you to these weirdos."

She cringed at the nickname he'd fashioned for her years ago. She didn't used to hate it, but she'd given up her obsession with baseball long ago. That was kid-Gemma. Now she was adult-Gemma. A lot had changed between the two. He wouldn't know that, of course, but hearing the nickname still reminded her of how they were strangers now. So why did he affect her so much?

"Obviously, you already know Elise and Hallie." He pointed at the guy now leaning against the counter next to the sink. "That's my cousin, Brad."

"Hey." Brad flicked his hand up in a wave.

Tyler shifted his attention to a woman sitting at the island with tight blonde curls pulled into a high ponytail. "And that's my cousin, Bridget. We call her Beej."

Cousins. That explained the family resemblance. Gemma bobbed her head toward them both. "Nice to meet you."

Then Tyler gestured toward the brunette. "And this is Kendall. She's Elise's best friend, but she's practically like another sister."

How did Kendall feel about the title of honorary sister? Gemma held back a cringe as an unwanted memory flashed through her mind. A memory she'd tried for years to forget.

But she never did. How could she when nothing was ever the same again?

Chapter Four

Seven Years Earlier

July

Gemma paced her bedroom floor, kicking at a pile of Cassie's clothes laying in the middle of the room. For how perfect her sister always tried to appear to everyone, couldn't she at least learn to pick up her things? It was really annoying having to share a room with her sometimes.

A cacophony of voices carried up to her from the living room a floor below. Some laughter. Gemma was certain she could even hear Mrs. Carrington crying. The woman never did well when families moved away. It was incredible how much emotion she displayed at these going-away parties. Their expat community was close, but really, she took it to the extreme.

For once, however, Gemma felt like joining her.

She stopped in front of the full-length mirror leaning against the wall and tucked a dark curl back into her ponytail. It did little good.

Somewhere down below, Tyler mingled with the rest of their neighbors. He'd been occupied for almost the entire party. That was no surprise. The Abernathys were the guests of honor, and everyone wanted to get in one last conversation, one last hug, before the family boarded a plane back to Florida for good.

I can't believe he's actually leaving. Gemma hiccuped a small sob. Saying goodbye without showing too much emotion had become one of her talents after growing up in a foreign country. It was normal for families to leave in this community. But somehow, it had never crossed her mind that she'd have to say goodbye to her best friend. She stifled another sob.

Gemma dropped onto her bed, checking the clock on her night-stand. Had she really been up here for an hour? It was already after eleven. If she didn't claim her time with him soon, she'd miss her chance. And she had something very important to tell him. Something she'd held inside for far too long.

"It's no big deal," she muttered, shaking out her fingers the way she always did when her nerves bubbled out of control. "Just three little words. 'I love you.'" The words came out squeaky and unnatural.

Her parents would freak if they knew what she wanted to say to him. "*Teenagers don't have enough life experience to know what real love is.*" Gemma had heard Mom tell Cassie that very thing last year when she'd come home crying over Peter Anderson—the guy she'd been crushing on for all of twenty-one days—leaving for college. That had only lasted a few weeks before she'd moved on to her next "true love."

But for Gemma, there had only been Tyler. And she didn't need any more life experience to understand her feelings about him.

She rolled her shoulders a few times, attempting to relax her posture. "Tyler, ever since the day you walked into my life, you've had my heart." Ew, gross. Way too desperate. The other kids in the neighborhood already teased her for talking older than a sixteen-year-old. She groaned, dropping her head into her hands. "Why is this so hard?" Her head jerked up, nose scrunching. "And why am I talking to myself?" Clearly, she'd lost it.

Rising from her bed, Gemma resumed pacing the floor. This was Tyler. He'd never once belittled anything about her. When the other kids had teased her about her brains or her clothes or her uncontrollable hair, he'd always accepted her for who she was, no matter what.

Losing her heart to him had been inevitable from the beginning. Even if he didn't feel the same.

"Oh, please feel the same." She threw her hands up in the air. There she went talking to herself again.

A set of five syncopated knocks rattled the window. Tyler's

knock. She turned to find her best friend's face pressed against the glass, one arm draped around the tree at the side of her house.

Gemma's heart did its own syncopated rhythm, and she went to let him inside. "You know there are these things called stairs," she said as he pulled himself through the window. "Why don't you ever use them?"

He'd often climbed over the tree between their yards to get in when he was supposed to be in his room doing homework. It annoyed his mother to no end whenever she discovered him gone, though Gemma usually managed to convince him to go back before he got caught.

"Where's the fun in that?" He flashed his dimpled grin her way.

Even with a mouth full of braces, it still managed to turn her knees to mush. She sank onto the window seat before her legs gave out completely.

"Plus, Mrs. Carrington's hugs were starting to suffocate me. She kept coming back for more. They're so tight I swear my eyes were about to bug out of my head."

Gemma laughed. "I guess it's a good thing my family will never leave so I won't have to experience a Mrs. Carrington farewell."

"Count yourself lucky, Slugger. They're not for the faint of heart. What're you doing up here anyway?"

Just talking myself off the ledge. "It was getting a little crowded downstairs. I needed a break from it all." Not to mention trying to keep herself from bursting into tears at the constant reminder of his approaching departure.

"I don't blame you." Tyler snatched her baseball glove and ball from her dresser and sprawled onto his back on her bed.

Gemma watched him toss the ball up, almost reaching the ceiling before gravity did its thing, and he caught it inches from his face. The repeated motion was strangely soothing, and for a moment, it seemed like any old night together—her lounging on the window seat doing homework while Tyler went to great lengths to avoid his. Any minute now, her mother would barge in and force them to come downstairs to try her mediocre attempt at some inde-cipherable Chilean cooking. Mom had a brilliant mind when it came to astronomy, but her kitchen skills needed work.

This wasn't a normal night though. And soon, Tyler would be gone. Gemma couldn't let that happen without telling him how she felt. Her bedroom wasn't the most ideal place for this conversation, not with Cassie's dirty clothes all over the floor. But at least they were alone. No one would be around to witness the awkward after-math if he didn't feel the same way she did.

Oh, please feel the same, she pleaded again, silently this time. Her nerves jumped. They reminded her of those poppers they played around with every Fourth of July. Tyler used to throw a bunch down on the ground at once when she least expected to startle her. Then he'd run away laughing, the sound so infectious that Gemma couldn't help joining in.

"Ty, I need to tell you something." She bit her lip, trying to find the right words for this confession. She could string together eloquent phrases and sentences to fill up pages of prose for her English classes. Why was it so hard to speak from her heart? "Something I haven't told anyone before. Ever."

"Have you been keeping secrets, Slug?" He tossed the ball into the air again, overshooting it this time. The contact with the ceiling changed its direction, making it land out of reach of his outstretched glove. Far from disappointed, he turned onto his side and propped his head onto his hand. "I thought we told each other everything."

"We do." Almost everything anyway. And soon there truly wouldn't be any secrets left. She shifted uncomfortably in the window seat. "I just don't really know how to tell you what I'm about to say."

The teasing smirk left his mouth, and he sat up, facing her and bracing his hands on his knees. "Come on, Gem. You know you can tell me anything."

Gemma took a steadying breath. "Okay, here goes—"

The bedroom door burst open, cutting off the words on the tip of her tongue. Cassie entered, her light blonde curls bouncing on her shoulders like a wave of gold. How she managed to tame her wild hair to make it look like that was a mystery to Gemma. She touched her own dark curls, which always seemed to look like she'd stuck her finger in a light socket. Ponytails were her best friend. Besides Tyler, of course.

"There you are, Gemma. Tyler is looking ..." She trailed off when she noticed him on her bed. "Oh, I guess he found you." Her eyes traveled to the lacy purple bra lying on the floor at his feet. Pink tinged her cheeks, and she slowly crossed to it, nudging it under the bed with her foot. "You know Mom hates it when we let boys come up here. Especially with the door closed."

Correction: Mom hated it when *Cassie* attempted to bring boys up to the room. She'd never voiced any concern about Tyler being in here. Which, come to think of it, didn't reflect flattering things about Gemma's social life. Her sister, on the other hand, was a completely different story.

They didn't talk much about Cassie's ... extracurricular activities ... but that didn't stop Gemma from overhearing the gossip about her sister's loose lips from all the other kids at their international school. All the girls wanted to be her, and the boys ... Well, they only wanted to make out with her. Gemma tried not to pay attention to it. She loved her sister, no matter her reputation.

"Yep, he found me." She shared an amused look with her best friend as Cassie tried to inconspicuously dispose of the clothes on the floor. At least he didn't worship at her sister's feet like everyone else.

Tyler rose from the bed and joined Gemma on the window seat. "What was it you wanted to tell me?"

She refused to lay her soul bare in front of Cassie. She hadn't even mentioned her crush to her twin out of fear that she'd overreact. Cassie was always trying to get Gemma to act more girly. Admitting to something as silly as liking a boy would only add kindling to that brush fire.

She bumped Tyler's arm. "Do you want to take a walk?"

"Sure."

They rose from the window, crossing the room. "See ya, Cass," he said, nudging her arm with the back of his hand as he passed her.

"Bye," Cassie replied, flashing her winning smile in his direction. "I'm still going to claim that hug before you leave. Don't forget."

The side of his mouth twitched up in a crooked smile. "I won't."

"What was that about?" Gemma asked after they'd left the room.

Tyler shrugged a shoulder. "Oh, nothing. We were just talking earlier. She made me promise I wouldn't leave without saying goodbye."

An uncomfortable feeling nagged at Gemma's stomach, but she decided to let the subject drop. They descended the stairs onto the main floor landing. The living room was still full of people despite the late hour. She spotted Mrs. Carrington nearby, dabbing at her eyes with a tissue while embracing Tyler's sister. Elise appeared as though she'd like to be anywhere else but having the life squeezed out of her by the neighborhood busybody.

Tyler snorted. "Go." He shoved Gemma gently to get her to move. "Let's get out of here before she sees us."

They laughed as they made their escape into the chilly darkness outside the house. She wrapped her arms around herself, attempting to trap in any warmth she could. Why hadn't she thought to grab a jacket?

"I think I've finally gotten used to the fact that it's cold in July here," Tyler said as they headed in the direction of the chest-high stucco wall running between their houses." He easily pulled himself up onto the wall and straddled it, his legs hanging down both sides. "It took long enough, right?"

Gemma stepped onto the large rock on the ground next to the wall and hopped up to sit beside him. "Right in time to move to a sweltering hot summer. Go figure." Once again, the reality that he was leaving in the morning hit her. She doubted their relationship would end simply because his family was moving away. It just wouldn't be the same.

"Miami is always hot. But yeah, it'll be weird. I guess I won't need this anymore." He flicked the collar of his gray jacket to cover his neck. "Are you going to come visit me?"

"I'll beg my parents until they give in and buy me a plane ticket." She forced a smile, hopefully masking how much her heart hurt.

"You better." He gave her knee a squeeze.

Gemma kicked her legs against the stucco. They'd sat like this so many times over the years that she'd lost count. "It's crazy to think we won't ever be able to meet out here after tonight."

"Yeah." Tyler swung his leg over the wall, bringing them shoulder to shoulder. He looked around the dark yard. The faint light from the house illuminated his profile, showing the slight bob of his Adam's apple when he swallowed.

The air turned thick between them. She didn't want her last moments with him to be filled with melancholy. "Don't tell me you're going to miss this place. You weren't exactly thrilled to be here when you first moved in." She poked his side with one finger.

Tyler wiggled away from her touch, laughing. "It's grown on me." He flashed her a grin that didn't quite meet his eyes. Just as quickly, it faded. "A lot of that is because of you. I'm going to miss you, Slugger."

Gemma couldn't have asked for a better opening if she'd written the script herself. "I'm going to miss you too." Her nerves raged again, and she took a breath. "Ty, I really need to—"

"I mean, it's not fair," he said, not realizing she'd spoken. "You're practically family. It's like I'm losing one of my sisters."

Sister? He thought of her as his sister? Gemma's whole body went cold as if someone had pushed her into Lago Grey. She'd never actually swam in the glacial lake in Patagonia—that was forbidden. But she imagined it would feel a lot like the icy chill engulfing her now.

How humiliating. All these years hiding her feelings, scared of ruining their friendship if she let her love show, she'd at least held out some hope that maybe he looked at her with some amount of amorous affection.

That hope died in less than a second.

She forced out a stuttering laugh. "Yeah. I totally get that. I feel the same way." If Tyler were her brother, Gemma wanted a new family.

Moments ago, she was heartbroken to say goodbye to him. Now, the aching in her chest was due to an entirely different reason.

And she needed to get away from him before the emotion spilled out of her completely.

Chapter Five

It was almost dark by the time they pulled into the parking lot of the movie theater. Tyler slowed to let a group of teen boys cross in front of the car.

"Keep your eyes peeled for a spot," he said, watching one of them kick the heel of the guy in front of him, tripping him up a bit. The friend retaliated by shoving him backward, then hurried off to join the long line weaving its way toward the ticket booth.

Tyler chuckled as he continued driving past the crowd lining up to purchase tickets. Flashing red and yellow lights rotating around the name of the theater on the awning stood out in harsh contrast to the increasing twilight.

"The Marquee Cinemas at Buena Hills," Gemma read quietly from the passenger seat.

Tyler glanced at her out of the corner of his eye, watching her take in the scene outside the car, her mouth slightly open in surprise. He got it. The Marquee Cinemas at Buena Hills, or just The Cinemas to the locals, was a shock at first sight. One of the oldest buildings in town, it looked like it had come straight out of a set from one of those Wild West movies and plopped in the middle of a modern California suburb. With only two screens and movies rotating on a weekly basis, the selection wasn't great, so the weekend crowds always took a visitor by surprise.

"A pretty swanky name for a place that hasn't been updated since the 1950s, huh?" Brad said, leaning forward from the back, bracing his hands on the front seats. He'd spent most of the short ride in that position, asking random questions to Gemma that, surprisingly, had made her laugh.

She turned her attention away from the scene outside to answer him. "I like it. It's quaint."

"A bigger theater opened a few years ago on the other side of town, but they can't beat Free Popcorn Fridays," Tyler informed her. "I'm pretty sure that's how this place stays in business. As long as you don't mind spending your night with a bunch of high schoolers."

He wasn't exaggerating. The majority of those waiting for tickets couldn't have been more than eighteen. At least half of those were probably too young to drive.

"Mmmm." That was all Gemma said before turning back to the window.

Tyler frowned. Why did she seem so reluctant to be around him? Part of him wondered if the only reason she'd agreed to ride with him was because the girls' car was full, and she didn't know the way to the theater. Not a very flattering assessment of her opinion of him obviously.

It wouldn't be like this if she'd just answered my calls, he grumbled silently as he turned into another row on his search for an allusive spot. Why had they drifted so far apart?

Brad thumped him on the shoulder and pointed straight ahead of them. "There's one up there. Hurry, before someone else takes it."

Tyler sped up a bit and pulled into the spot in front of a navy sedan coming the other way. An angry honk pierced the darkness, and he looked out the rearview mirror to find Hallie and Kendall gesturing at him from the passenger side of the other car.

"Ha ha! Suckers!" Brad let out a hearty guffaw. Then, speaking as though they could hear him, he said, "Better luck next time."

Tyler had barely pulled the keys from the ignition before Gemma's door was open, and she'd jumped out of the car as if she couldn't get away fast enough. Brad slid out a second later, still chuckling about the cleverness of cutting the girls off.

Alone in the car, Tyler drummed his fingers on the steering wheel and puffed out his cheeks. This wasn't working. As much as he'd wanted to see Gemma again—that's what he'd wanted for years, really—maybe inviting her to go to the movie with them hadn't been the best idea. She obviously didn't want to be there, and it seemed that nothing he said or did was going to change that. Letting the breath out more forcefully than he'd intended, he sat for a few more seconds before joining Brad on the pavement.

"Dude, I thought you said Gemma was your best friend," his cousin said in an undertone once she was far enough away not to overhear.

Tyler watched her wander over to the girls, who'd found a spot in the next row and were walking in the direction of the theater, laughing about something.

"She used to be." He left it at that.

Elise reached out and linked arms with Gemma like they were old friends. That only confused him more. Why would Gemma act all buddy-buddy with his sisters, but treat him like a stranger? She even seemed more comfortable around Brad. Which, for the record, should just not happen.

Puzzling over that question, he shoved his hands into his pockets and started toward the others. Brad fell into step beside him.

"I could be wrong here," he said, his tone casual, "but aren't friends supposed to talk to each other? The way I see it, it kind of seems like she thinks you're from another planet." He caught Tyler's side-eye and stepped back, both hands up in surrender. "Like I said, I could be wrong."

Tyler ran a hand down the front of his face and sighed. "Here's the thing. It's been seven years since I've seen her. I didn't expect to jump right in like everything was the same between us after all this time, but I hoped that she'd at least be happy to see me."

"Hm ..." Brad put a hand to his chin in a very good impression of that famous statue of the thinking man. "Don't worry, bruh. I'll get to the bottom of this." And he trotted off to catch up to the others.

"*Brad,*" Tyler hissed, lunging for him with both hands outstretched, but his cousin was too quick, and he only grabbed air.

He pulled a hand back to rub at the nape of his neck, then followed Brad, dragging his feet.

He reached the rest of the group right as Brad squeezed in between Gemma and Elise, throwing his arms around both their shoulders with about as much finesse as a tornado trapped in a small wooden shack. "So, Gemma, why aren't you talking to Tyler?"

Tyler stopped in his tracks at the same time that Gemma reared back, her eyebrows shooting up as high as they could go.

Beej gasped, and Hallie let out a long, disgusted groan. A strong temptation to flee the scene came over him. *Thanks a lot, pal,* he thought, shooting a glare at his cousin. Now Gemma would know they'd been talking about her.

"Excuse me?" she asked. The single word wobbled with a surprised laugh.

"What the heck, Brad," Elise said, giving him her own look of disapproval before Gemma could say anything more. "Why would you ask something like that?"

He shrugged, a smirk appearing on his mouth. "What? It's a valid question." He turned back to Gemma but slung his arm around Tyler's shoulder, patting him on the chest with his free hand. "Why aren't you talking to my cousin, here?"

Her cheeks had turned a deep shade of scarlet. Tyler didn't think he'd ever seen her blush like that. "Of course I'm talking to him. What makes you think I'm not?" She pursed her lips together and slowly lifted her eyes to meet his, a mixture of confusion and pleading in her gaze that cut right through him. It was a look he knew well. She needed him to run interference.

Pushing his own embarrassment aside, he stepped next to Beej and nodded toward the leather purse hanging from her shoulder. It had to be the largest purse he'd ever seen, about the size of a small duffel bag. A bulky beige sweater exploded out of the top. "I see you have your Mary Poppins bag with you tonight."

The comment had exactly the result he'd hoped. The focus shifted away from Gemma as everyone turned to the bag in question.

Out of the corner of his eye, he glimpsed the relieved look that flashed across Gemma's face.

Beej patted her purse lovingly. "It wouldn't be a night at the movies without it."

Brad bent his head toward her, dropping his voice so those outside of their circle wouldn't hear him. "What kind of treats you got in there?"

Pulling her sweater out, Beej handed it to her brother, then held the bag open so he could peek inside. "I've got licorice and jelly-beans, a few kinds of candy bars. Oh, and Sour Patch Kids. But those are Elise's, so if you want some, you'll have to suck up to her."

It wouldn't be a trip to the movies without Beej and her magic bag. She always claimed that the reason she snuck in food was to fight against the injustice of how much theaters charged for snacks. *"You have to sell a whole kidney in order to see a single movie,"* she'd once exclaimed while stuffing her purse with all her favorites.

But everyone knew the real reason she did it so gleefully. This was the only way the always rule-abiding Bridget Lucas ever bent the law. Not that sneaking food into a movie constituted an actual crime, which was probably why she did it. She snuck anything that would fit into her seemingly bottomless bag. Candy. Burgers and fries. Soda. Once, she'd even managed to get an entire pizza past the pimply-faced teenager checking the tickets. They all still talked about that one.

"That's impressive," Gemma admitted, growing more comfort-able by the minute. "I guess I've been going to movies the wrong way my entire life."

Brad nudged her. "Stick with us, we'll show you how to do a lot of things the right way."

What the heck did he mean by that? Gemma appeared not to know as well. Instead of responding, her eyes flicked to Tyler's again, full of questions.

"So, what are you in the mood for?" he asked, again changing the subject. The sooner they got to their seats where they didn't have to talk, the better. They'd almost reached the front of the line. He pointed to the marquee above the awning displaying the two movies currently playing. "Car chases and explosions or kissing and romance? Take your pick, Slugger."

Something flashed across her face, but she followed his hand to look at the selections. When she turned to him again, whatever reaction she'd given him had vanished. With a decisive nod of her head, she said, "Definitely explosions."

Chapter Six

Gemma had a hard time waking up the next morning. The sun was already streaming into her room when she opened her eyes, and a gentle breeze rustled the leaves of the oak tree outside her open window. She stifled a yawn, rolling over to face the wall and snuggling deeper under the green-and-white patchwork quilt. A few more minutes in bed wouldn't hurt after staying out so late.

The movie hadn't let out until after eleven, and by the time she'd endured the uncomfortable ride back to Tyler's house to get her car, it was close to midnight before she'd made it home. Gemma was no night owl. She could never muster enough desire to stay up late enough to greet a new year, let alone a random Saturday.

She'd crept into the dark house so she wouldn't wake Gram and had only managed to change out of her clothes before dragging her tired body into bed, hoping to fall asleep right away. In the quiet stillness of her room, however, her mind had refused to stop analyzing the entire evening, and hours removed from the ordeal, her face still burned at the blunt way Brad had asked, "Why aren't you talking to Tyler?"

How was she supposed to answer that question? There was no way she was going to air her issues with Tyler in front of his family. If it weren't for Beej and her humongous bag of contraband snacks, there was no knowing what would have come out of Gemma's mouth.

Usually, when faced with a situation in which she didn't know what to say, the perfect response always came to her hours later, like a giant light bulb going off, and she'd wish to return to the moment to deliver the unexpected mic drop and shock everyone in attendance. But even now, she had no snappy comeback.

At least she'd made it through with most of her dignity intact. And now that it was over, she could put the whole night behind her and go back to focusing on helping Gram and looking for a job.

She wasn't sure how long she lay snuggled underneath her blankets or if she'd managed to drift off to sleep again before a long, repeated buzzing punctured the silence. With a groan, she rolled over and snatched her phone off the nightstand, accepting the video chat from her sister.

"Hey." Cassie's face lit up as cheerfully as the small swatch of robin's-egg blue from the sky behind her. "You're still in bed? Are you feeling okay?"

Reluctantly, Gemma pulled herself into a sitting position and balanced her phone on her knees. "It's not that late here, Cass. You're three hours ahead of me." She checked the time on the upper corner of the screen to be sure. A quarter after nine? Okay, maybe her sister's concern wasn't so off base. "I'm fine. I was out late last night with some people."

"Yeah?" Cassie asked, talking loudly to be heard over the sounds of the Big Apple pinging off the walls of the buildings around her. "You spend so much time helping Gram. I worry you don't get to meet many people. But yay! You're making friends!"

Friends was a bit of a stretch, but Gemma didn't comment. She wasn't about to bring up the fact that she'd been with Tyler. She hadn't talked about him for years, especially with Cassie. She'd rather not run the risk of digging up past demons. Not when her relationship with her twin was so much better now.

"Where are you going?" she asked instead.

"I'm meeting Drew for lunch at our favorite sushi place." Cassie seemed to be walking fast, judging by the breathy quality of her words. "I should've been there an hour ago, but Adriana had me running errands all morning. And then the barista messed up her order—"

"Don't you ever get the weekends off?" Gemma asked.

"The fashion industry never sleeps, especially in New York."

Cassie had said that many times since landing a position as the assistant for Adriana Escarra, one of New York's hot, up-and-coming designers.

Gemma stifled another yawn. "And … you're still happy there?"

Cassie offered what would appear to anyone else to be a carefree smile. But Gemma, who knew her sister better than anyone in the entire world, saw something underneath its brightness. Something forced. "Of course! I'm living the dream."

So why didn't it sound like it?

In the last six months, her sister had spoken more about dry cleaning and her boss's preferences for imported coffee than anything related to fashion. She sounded more like a glorified errand runner. But Cassie had always insisted it was worth it.

"I have to work my way up from the ground floor," she'd said every time Gemma had expressed any kind of concern. "Someday, I'll make it on my own." For her sister's sake, Gemma hoped that was true.

"And anyway," Cassie continued, "Adriana is already giving me two weeks off for my trip to Mexico."

A loud siren blared angrily behind her, drowning out anything else she could've said.

"You're going to Mexico?" Gemma asked once the background noise had dimmed to a steady hum from the heavy traffic inching through the streets.

Cassie beamed, the excitement radiating from her smile. "Drew surprised me with it a few days ago. He planned the whole thing. He even talked my boss into giving me the time off. I don't think I would've managed it myself."

Drew's father owned the fancy law firm on Manhattan's Upper West Side that represented Adriana Escarra. The same firm that Drew had been working at for the past two years since passing the bar. His prior connection had helped Cassie land her job in the first place.

"And that's not all." It didn't seem possible for Cassie to glow any more than she was already, but somehow, she managed it. "I'm pretty sure Drew is going to propose while we're there."

"What?" Gemma bolted upright, throwing off her quilt, which tumbled to the floor. "Cassie! You didn't tell me you were thinking about getting engaged."

"I know, I know," Cassie said regretfully. "I didn't want to jinx it. But we've been talking a lot about it lately, and he's been dropping some serious hints about doing it soon."

Gemma felt a smile spread across her face as she reached down to pick the quilt off the floor. She tossed it back onto the bed, then swung her legs over the side and placed her feet on the plush carpet. There would be no going back to sleep after this piece of news. "I'm so excited for you. You better tell me all about it when you get back."

"I will for sure. And I expect you to come to New York when I shop for my wedding dress. There's no way I'm picking out *the one* without my sister there."

"Just tell me when and where," Gemma said as a warm, cinna-mony smell wafted into her room. *Gram must be making French toast.* A twinge of guilt pierced her stomach for not being downstairs to help with breakfast. "I think Gram is up. I should go downstairs. I feel bad sleeping this late."

Another siren wailed on Cassie's end, accompanied by a series of car honks. "How is Gram?"

Gemma shrugged. "Oh, you know how she is. Still thinking she can take on the whole world even at seventy-five. I have to constantly tell her it's okay to rest. She won't listen."

That made Cassie laugh. "I still think you should try to convince her to sell the house."

"You know as well as I do that she won't do that. Dad's been pestering her to move closer to them since the funeral. She won't budge." Gemma glanced at herself in the mirror, grimacing at the sorry state of her curls. She propped her phone on top of her dresser, then grabbed the hair tie next to it, gathering her locks into a frizzy ponytail. "I can't say I blame her though. It would be hard to let go of the place she's lived in her entire married life."

The possibility of selling the house had been a topic of conversation for years, ever since Mom and Dad had moved back to Oregon after Gemma and Cassie graduated from high school. But although Gram and Grandpa differed in so many ways, they were both blessed with an equal dose of stubbornness. No one could convince them to leave their beloved house. And now that Grandpa was gone, Gram only grew more adamant about staying.

"She could come live with me," Cassie said brightly.

Gemma snorted, then covered her mouth with her hand. "Yeah right. Can you picture Gram in New York?"

"There's a first for everything. She and I would take the city by storm."

That made Gemma laugh harder. "I think *you'd* have an easier time convincing a fish it's a bird than getting Gram to come to New York."

Cassie made a noise of contemplation. "You're probably right. I just worry about her sometimes in that house all alone. I mean, what's going to happen when you leave? It's not like you're planning to live with her forever, right? What if you meet someone?"

"I don't know," Gemma admitted honestly. She hadn't really thought about much past the start of her master's program. "It's not like I have to worry about that right now since I don't know anyone."

Cassie hummed. "To be honest, I was shocked when you called it off with Blake. He seemed like a really good fit for you. I was already hoping for a double wedding." She flashed a grin that Gemma only returned halfheartedly.

"He *was* good," Gemma said. "And I really liked him. Something just didn't click."

On paper, her on-again, off-again boyfriend of the last three years had checked all the boxes: kind, intelligent, driven, with a sense of humor that had her laughing so hard she couldn't breathe.

Once he'd even made her shoot milk out of her nose. And yet, though she couldn't put her finger on it, something had been missing. She'd tried to ignore it, but the nagging uncertainty had finally won out, and she'd called it quits for good right before moving to Buena Hills.

"Well, I know someone amazing is destined for your future," Cassie responded. "How could there not be? Any guy would be beyond lucky to win you over."

Gemma was touched by the compliment. They'd come a long way since that horrible night seven years ago before Tyler moved back to Florida. She didn't think she'd ever be able to forgive her sister after the way she …

Nope, she wouldn't go there. Gemma had worked too hard to forget about it. Seeing Tyler again was simply bringing it to the surface. She didn't want a reason to go back to resenting her sister.

Before she could respond, Cassie's attention was diverted by something off the screen. Her elated smile could only mean one thing. A second later, her words confirmed it. "Hey, heartthrob. Sorry I'm late. Adriana had me running around all morning." After giving Drew a kiss—off camera, thankfully—she addressed Gemma again. "I gotta go, sis. I'll call you later."

"Eat some sushi for me, okay?" Gemma responded.

Cassie scrunched her nose. "You hate sushi."

Gemma laughed. "Enjoy your trip, if I don't talk to you before then."

"I will. But we're not leaving for two weeks. I'll for sure talk to you before then. Tootles!"

Cassie hung up before Gemma had a chance to say goodbye. She was always that way. Once she'd wrapped up one task, or emotion, or experience, it was full steam ahead to the next one.

If only Gemma could be more like that. Instead, she clung to things way longer than was healthy for a normal person. She frowned at herself in the mirror. "You're not being fair to yourself," she muttered to her reflection.

Perhaps she was only unsettled over coming face-to-face with

Tyler again after all this time. That had to be why she was being bombarded by all this uncertainty.

Determining to be kinder to herself from now on, she placed her phone on the dresser and left her room. She wouldn't give Tyler another thought. She'd rather focus on the smell of Gram's cinnamon French toast beckoning her down the stairs.

Chapter Seven

On Tuesday afternoon, Tyler clocked out of his shift at the campus bookstore and returned to the one cubicle allotted to the shipping department to grab his bag. The two guys who'd just arrived for work already occupied the small space.

Tyler stopped a few steps away, tilting his head slightly to one side in amusement when he saw Landon sitting in the swivel chair, spinning wildly. Aaron, his hip perched against the desk, counted out loud enthusiastically while looking at his watch. Neither of them noticed Tyler's approach.

He bit his bottom lip. Oh, he could have some fun with this. In his best impression of their boss, he said in a raspy voice, "Are you working hard … or hardly working?"

Both men jumped—Tyler laughed hard when Landon almost fell out of the chair—bringing an abrupt end to their game.

Aaron slugged Tyler hard on the shoulder. "I hate it when you do that. You sound just like him."

"That's why I do it," he said. "You both are so easy."

Their boss wasn't strict by any definition of the word, but he did expect them to make themselves useful, even when they weren't given a specific assignment.

Landon leaned back in the chair, crossing his arms over his chest. "You taking off?"

"Yeah, I have a class." Tyler squeezed past the chair and picked up his backpack from the floor in the corner, slinging it over his shoulder. "Don't forget, if any old ladies ask for your number over the phone, don't give it to them."

Aaron threw his head back and roared with laughter. Landon

only rolled his eyes. "That happened one time, and I didn't give it to her."

"You have to admit you thought about it," Aaron joked, amusement still written across his face.

"I did not!" Landon flicked a pen at his coworker who shot his hand up to catch it before being nailed in the face. "She sounded old enough to be my grandma."

Tyler chuckled as he slid his other arm through the strap of his backpack. "See ya, fellas." He touched his temple with his pointer finger, then flicked it forward in a sideways peace sign before turning and walking away. A few farewells, and a couple of jokes punctuated by laughter, followed him out of the stockroom.

He entered the main floor of the bookstore, heading for the front exit. As he passed the section for women's apparel, his eyes landed on Gemma browsing through a rack of sweatshirts. She pulled one out and showed it to the elderly woman standing next to her. Despite never meeting her in person, he'd seen enough pictures while growing up with Gemma to know he was standing before the infamous Grandma June. She looked older now, though no less spry than Gemma had described her.

Tyler hesitated, unsure whether he should approach or pretend he hadn't seen them and keep walking. With the way she'd acted around him at the movie on Friday, he doubted she'd want to see him now.

Stop. You're overthinking it. She's still your friend.

Maybe she'd been tired that night. He was never himself whenever he didn't get enough sleep. And moving across states would wear out even the most energetic person. Besides, any reunion after seven years was bound to be awkward. It wouldn't get better if he didn't put in a little effort. Pushing aside his hesitation, he pasted on a smile and approached them. "Hey, Slugger."

Gemma's head jerked in his direction, her eyebrows shooting upward. "Tyler."

Her surprise alerted Grandma June, who then placed the T-shirt she'd been examining back on the rack. "Gemma, dear, introduce me to this nice young man here."

Gemma pursed her lips before turning to her grandma. "This is Tyler. He's a ... friend. From Chile."

Tyler didn't miss her hesitation on the word *friend*.

Grandma June—Mrs. Schalk—however, wasn't shy at all. "Oh, I thought you looked familiar. You're even more handsome in person than all the pictures Gemma has shown me."

Handsome? He liked her already.

"My Gemma used to talk about you constantly every time she came to visit," Mrs. Schalk continued. "It was always Tyler this, and Tyler and me that. She was quite heartbroken when your family moved back to the States."

A blush appeared on Gemma's face. "*Graaaam.*"

"It's very nice to finally meet you, Mrs. Schalk." He held out his hand.

The woman placed her wrinkled hand in his, waving the other off to the side. "Oh please. None of this Mrs. Schalk business. Not with such a good friend of my granddaughter's. You're practically family. You can call me Grandma June."

Tyler bobbed his head slowly, glancing at Gemma to gauge her reaction to her grandmother's statement. She seemed to be doing her best *not* to meet his eye. He returned his attention to Grandma June. "I'd be honored. What brings you lovely ladies to the bookstore today?"

It was Grandma June who spoke. "Gemma accompanied me to my doctor's appointment nearby, and we stopped in for a few minutes on our way to lunch. My granddaughter is in serious need of some spirit wear. Now that she's in Trojan country, it's time for her to put away that silly yellow and green nonsense."

Tyler tapped Gemma's forearm with the back of a single finger. "She's right, you know."

Gemma shook her head, though her mouth twitched in the beginning of a tiny, reluctant smile. "Not going to happen. I'll wear the shirt to appease you people, but I'll always be a Duck."

"Shhhh," he hissed, putting a finger over his lips and looking around with wild eyes. "Don't let anyone around here hear you say that."

Grandma June laughed. "Why don't you join us for lunch, Tyler?" She linked arms with him, catching him by surprise.

He patted the woman's hand where it rested in the crook of his arm. "I wish I could. Unfortunately, I have to get to calculus." He grimaced. "I need all the help I can get to pass my test coming up."

"You still don't like math?" Gemma asked.

"No. And it doesn't like me either."

Grandma June chuckled as she pulled her arm away. "My Gemma is a whiz at math. She graduated summa cum laude. Did you know?"

Gemma's face flushed at the praise. She'd always had a hard time with compliments. Apparently, that hadn't changed.

"She didn't mention it," he said, smiling. "You were always smarter than the rest of us. Remember that time Henry Parker dubbed you The Brilliant One and tried to convince you to do his homework?" Henry had been a year ahead of them at their international school in Santiago.

"He was shocked when I didn't fall for it." She gestured to herself with both hands. "Hello, top scores in the whole school."

"Well, Henry was never very bright."

Gemma laughed hard at that, sending a wave of relief through him.

"Did I ever tell you about his sister's wedding planner phase? That was before you moved in. She forced Henry and me to be the bride and groom." She shuddered.

"Only about a dozen times," Tyler teased. "The word around the street is that it was a lovely wedding."

Gemma smacked his arm, a playful smile lighting her face and sending something zipping through him he'd never felt before. At least not around her.

"I never liked him," she continued. "He was always such a jerk to me. Making fun of my hair or teasing me because of my grades. He was the one who convinced the other boys not to let me play ball with them."

Tyler wasn't a big fan of him either. "What an oaf. You showed them though. You threw harder than any of us."

"Yeah, thanks to you." Gemma seemed to grow more comfortable with him the longer they talked about the good old days. "They never would've let me play if you hadn't threatened to slice through the leather of their baseball gloves."

"I would've done it too." He glanced at his watch, sucking a breath in through his teeth. "I gotta go. Professor Boyd locks the door when he starts the class. And I need a good grade on the test on Friday if I want to have a chance at passing this class."

Grandma June shot him a commiserating look and held out her hand. "It was a pleasure meeting you, Tyler Abernathy."

He gave her fingers a gentle squeeze. "The pleasure is absolutely mine. I hope to see you again soon."

Her look of approval changed to a pointed one directed at her granddaughter. Gemma answered with a slight shake of the head so small it almost went unnoticed. Tyler knew the look of a silent conversation when he saw one. And this conversation obviously didn't include him. He started to leave.

"Tyler," Gemma said when he'd only gone two steps. He turned back around. She studied him blankly for a few seconds, then sighed. "What are you doing tomorrow night?"

He shrugged. "I don't have plans."

"Why don't you come over and I'll"—her shoulders slumped a bit as if she were about to suggest something she didn't want to but felt she had no choice—"help you study for your test."

"Are you serious?" After being so reluctant to be around him the other day? Maybe talking about their old school foe had broken the ice. *I'll have to send Henry a thank-you card.*

Gemma looked at her grandma, who urged her on with an eager nod of her head. "Yeah."

"Then I'll be there." He lightly punched her shoulder. "Thanks, Slugger. You're a lifesaver."

Chapter Eight

"What in the world is all this?" Gemma asked, entering the kitchen the next evening. Gram looked up from the dish she was pulling out of the oven. The smell of her famous orange-pineapple ham filled the room.

Gemma's suspicions had risen as soon as she'd pulled up to their cute little craftsman bungalow. The familiar smells wafting from the house sent her catapulting back to her childhood when her family would turn into this exact driveway after a long day of travel. Gram always had a hearty meal and a warm smile waiting for them when they arrived.

Standing in the doorway of the kitchen, taking in Gram's guilty expression as she set the mouth-watering ham on the stove, Gemma's premonition skyrocketed. Her grandma was up to something.

"It's not every day my granddaughter has a handsome man-friend over," Gram responded. She adjusted the temperature of the oven before picking up the sheet of her uncooked brown oatmeal rolls and sliding them in.

Gemma shot her eyes to the ceiling before rubbing two fingers in the space between her brows. Even after her semi-normal conversation with Tyler in the bookstore yesterday, she'd regretted inviting him over before the words had even left her mouth. She knew the likelihood of avoiding him completely would be slim, but she certainly hadn't made things easier on herself by allowing him into her home.

"Gram, he's coming over to study. I didn't invite him for Christmas dinner." She gestured wildly at the scalloped potatoes and green bean casserole on the counter next to the stove. "Is this why you shooed me out of the house this afternoon?"

"I thought it would be easier for you to look for jobs away from home." Gram opened the cabinet to her left. "Be a dear and set the table please."

Gemma moved away from the doorway with a huff. "Everything is done online now. Where'd you get all this food anyway? You can't tell me you randomly keep a full-sized ham in your freezer." She'd seen inside of it. There wasn't room among all the frozen vegetables and the loaves of bread Gram still insisted on making every week.

Gram continued buzzing about her business as if being surrounded by all of Gemma's holiday favorites in April was a normal occurrence. "Mary, from next door, showed me this app where you can order whatever you want from the grocery store and have it delivered right to your door. Technology these days. What will they think of next?"

Gemma gave her a wry smile as she reached into the cabinet for plates. "Maybe now you can learn how to text. It's so much easier than ordering groceries. And you know Cassie would love that." Her sister rarely answered the phone when someone other than Gemma called, but she'd text back in a heartbeat.

"Now that's simply asking too much." Gram swatted her arm, drawing a laugh from Gemma, then turned back to pulling apart the individual slices of ham with a fork.

Gemma walked the plates to the table, jostling them a little as she set them down. The clanking of the ceramic drew Gram's attention.

"Careful, dear," she said over her shoulder. "Those are my good plates."

"Sorry." Gemma separated the dishes onto three place settings. "I guess I'm a little nervous." *And kicking myself for getting into this mess.*

She still didn't understand why a man she hadn't seen since she was a teenager was making her so flustered all the time. Was it because he'd been her best friend and she felt guilty for pulling away, or was she still bothered by the—

Nope. She refused to let herself go there. Not now when Tyler would be at her house any minute.

"You really didn't have to go through all this trouble," she said. "I'm sure he already ate." *And you'll wear yourself out.* Gemma didn't say that out loud. Although Gram still claimed to be in good health, her energy level wasn't up to what it used to be. Even if she constantly insisted otherwise, Gemma could tell she tired easily. Spending all afternoon in the kitchen had to be taxing on the woman.

"Young men are always hungry," Gram said, finally turning from the ham to fix her granddaughter with the no-nonsense look she always used when she was trying to convince someone she knew best. She crossed to Gemma, placing an arm around her shoulders. "And there's no reason to be nervous. Tyler seems like a good one. And cute. Almost makes me wish I were fifty years younger."

A laugh bubbled up from deep in Gemma's gut, escaping before she could stop it. "*Grandma.*"

Gram shrugged a shoulder in an *I said what I said, deal with it* gesture. Then she squeezed Gemma's arm. "Gather your courage, my dear. I expect he'll be here soon." The timer beeped, and she returned to the oven to take out the rolls.

"Not likely. He's always late," Gemma mumbled the words automatically.

She retrieved forks and knives from the drawer by the sink and set them next to the plates. She'd hardly placed the third set of silverware down when Gram picked up one of the plates and walked over to the stove.

"What are you doing?" Gemma asked.

Gram looked way too innocent for her own good. "You don't need me hanging around your date. I can eat this in my room."

Ugh. Leave it to Gram to put on her matchmaking hat tonight.

She took way too much interest in the love lives of her granddaughters. Was it too late for Gemma to cancel? Or at least tell Tyler to meet her somewhere?

But then she'd feel guilty that Gram had gone through so much trouble to cook all this food. Even if it had been unnecessary and entirely too much.

"It's not a date," Gemma insisted. "I'm helping him study."

Gram plopped a spoonful of scalloped potatoes onto her plate next to the slice of ham. "You young kids don't call them study dates for nothing."

Rolling her eyes, Gemma straightened the two place settings to give her hands something to do. "We don't have that kind of relationship. It's never been like that." Tyler had made it perfectly clear their relationship was strictly platonic. Not only platonic. Familial. *It's like I'm losing one of my sisters.* Too bad he didn't feel that same sense of familial connection with Cassie.

Gram pursed her lips, doing a terrible job of holding back a smile. "We'll see about that."

A knock punctured the nervous silence that followed. Gemma's heart stuttered in direct opposition to the dread settling in her stomach. She steeled herself for another uncomfortable evening with Tyler Abernathy.

Gram retrieved the third set of silverware from the table as she shuffled to the stairs. "I'll be in my room."

Gemma still didn't appreciate what Gram was doing. "You really don't have to leave. I'm sure Tyler wouldn't mind if you joined us."

At the foot of the stairs, Gram turned back. "No, no. You two go ahead. I'm feeling tired. I think I'll catch up on my shows and get an early night's rest. Tell that fine young man hello from me." She winked and disappeared up the stairs.

Gemma blew out a cleansing breath before leaving the kitchen, shaking out her hands as she walked through the living room to the front door. She stood for a moment with her fingers gripping the knob, taking some time to squash the nerves that were about to spill out.

At the second knock, her hand sprung back as if the silver knob were made of molten lava. Not wanting to appear too eager, she waited another few seconds. She *wasn't* eager to see him.

Not even a little bit.

When she finally opened the door, a wide smile split the bottom half of Tyler's face. Okay, maybe she was a tiny bit eager. But she wasn't happy about it.

"Hey, there you are," he said. "I was starting to wonder if I had the wrong house."

Gemma backed up to let him enter, shutting the door behind him. "Nope. You're in the right place. I was ... uh ..." *Just freaking out a little bit. No big deal.* She searched her mind for an excuse for taking so long. "Finishing up dinner. It was kind of a crucial part." Sure, she'd go with that, even if it weren't exactly true. Gram's timing in the kitchen was always impeccable. If she said dinner was at seven, the table would be set and food served at seven on the dot.

"No worries," Tyler said, flashing another one of his gorgeous smiles. "Thanks for having me over. I really appreciate you helping me study."

Her breath caught in her throat. *Get a grip, girl,* she thought, hoping he wouldn't notice the blush that had to be taking over her cheeks. She'd seen that smile hundreds of times before. It shouldn't still make her this dizzy with endorphins. "Are you hungry?"

"I could eat, but you don't need to feed me. Although it does smell amazing in here."

"It was no trouble," Gemma said over her shoulder as she led the way to the kitchen. *Especially since I didn't do anything.* "Gram likes to eat right at seven and be relaxing by eight, so ..."

They entered the kitchen, and Tyler's eyes fell on the two place settings, then flipped to the elaborate feast laid out on the stove and countertops. He turned to Gemma, his brows raised in question.

"What's the occasion? I feel underdressed. Should I go home and change into a suit?"

She twittered out a laugh she wished she could take back. "This is Gram's Christmas dinner menu. She never cooked it on Christmas, though, since it was always only her and my grandpa. She insisted on celebrating the holidays during the summer when we came to visit." Gemma felt another blush coming on, so she dropped her head and brought her hand up, resting her fist on her temple to block the side of her face from his view. "I think she's trying to make our study time into more of a study ... date."

"Oh." Tyler shoved his hands into the pockets of his jeans and looked around. An uncomfortable silence filled the room. Could he feel it, or was it only her? Their eyes met, and by the way he bounced on his heels slightly, Gemma was certain he did. Then his stomach growled, loud and unmistakable, and he chuckled. "I guess I'm hungrier than I thought."

"Come on, then. Let's eat." Gemma hurried to the table and picked up one of the plates. Her hands were shaking so much, it was a miracle she didn't drop the dish. At least Gram hadn't insisted on using the fine china she normally set out during Christmas dinner.

"Where's Grandma June?" Tyler asked, leaving his backpack on the floor near the table and picking up the second plate. He joined Gemma at the stove. "Is she not eating with us?"

"It's been a long day, so she wanted to lie down." She was too nervous to be hungry, but she couldn't resist her grandma's delicious cooking.

Tyler set his overflowing plate on the table and sat next to her. "Is she okay?"

"Oh yeah. She'll be fine after a little rest." Knowing Gram, she was probably lying on the floor with a cup to her ear attempting to eavesdrop on their conversation. Gemma snorted at the mental picture.

"What's so funny?" he asked, pausing with his fork in front of his mouth.

"Huh?" Gemma looked at him. "Oh, nothing. Sorry, I was just thinking." She took a bite of ham, savoring the delicious citrus flavors mingling in perfect harmony with the saltiness of the meat.

They ate in silence for a moment until Tyler nudged her with the back of his hand. "You know what this reminds me of?" He broke off a large piece of roll and stuffed it in his mouth.

"Hm?" Why did the slightest touch send sparks up her arm? This was so wrong.

Tyler didn't answer right away as he finished chewing. After swallowing, he said, "Remember when we were kids and used to crash each other's houses during mealtimes?"

Gemma smiled against her will. "My parents started setting an extra plate at the table in case you randomly showed up right as we were sitting down to eat." Which happened more often than not. He was a good sport when it came to Mom's questionable cooking skills.

He chuckled. "Mine did that too. You were as much a part of my family as I was."

"It's like I'm losing one of my sisters." Why couldn't she get that thought out of her head? It replayed again, successfully sinking the tiny bit of happiness percolating inside her. She forced herself to keep smiling, but it was tight.

Thankfully, Tyler didn't seem to notice. He cocked his head to the side as he considered her with a look Gemma had never seen on his face when aimed at her. What did it mean? Was she simply out of practice at reading him, or was there something else to it?

After a second, though, it vanished, and he spoke. "How's Cassie doing? I haven't talked to her in forever."

Gemma had wondered how long it would take him to ask about her twin. The question was posed innocently, but it still rubbed her the wrong way. Perhaps it was because she'd always thought Tyler indifferent to Cassie's charm. He'd seemed that way before *the incident.* But it turned out he'd been no different than all the other hot-blooded guys at her school. She pushed away the thought. She couldn't change the past, no matter how much she wanted to.

Still, she sawed off a piece of ham with more force than necessary. "She's good. Just living in New York, working for some fancy fashion designer." She shoved the bite into her mouth to disguise her frown.

Tyler leaned one elbow on the table, angling his body toward her. "I'm not at all surprised. That was her goal all along, wasn't it?"

"Of course. And Cassie always gets what she wants." Did that sound bitter? Gemma hadn't intended it to. But intentional or not, she spoke the truth. Cassie *did* always get what she wanted, sometimes even at the expense of everything and *everyone* else.

"What do you mean by that?" he asked, his brows drawing together.

"Nothing. Sorry."

They wouldn't solve anything by digging into past hurts now. She pushed the food around her plate, mortified at the stinging in her eyes.

"Are you okay?" he asked with an uncharacteristic softness in his tone.

I would be if you weren't here. Why was she even tempted to cry? She'd already grieved the loss of him. Having him back in her life was wreaking havoc on her emotions. She had to pull herself together.

"I'm fine," she said finally, pushing back her chair and walking her empty plate to the sink.

An awkward tension filled the kitchen as she worked to compose herself. Tyler remained at the table, probably wondering if she'd eaten some kind of rotten apple to make her act so weird. Was it too late to claim illness and bow out of the whole studying portion of this non-date?

Plucking the dish wand out of the bowl at the back of the sink, she turned on the faucet to break the silence and scrubbed the plate clean. The dishwasher would take care of the rest of the dishes, but she needed something to keep her shaking hands busy.

"Are you sure nothing's wrong?" he asked right behind her.

She jumped, whirling to face him. Water from the dish wand dribbled onto his shirt as the plate slipped from her hand.

Tyler snagged it before it tumbled to the floor, saving it from shattering to pieces. He had the reflexes of an athlete. Or former athlete. Gemma realized she had no idea if he even still played baseball.

After placing the plate in the sink where it was safe, he set both hands on her upper arms, then removed them quickly when she flinched. "Please," he pleaded. "Give me something. We used to be able to talk about everything."

Technically, he spoke the truth. But not *their* truth. His words applied to two children who were the best of friends. Not the adults who were strangers now.

She forced herself to look at him. "That was back when we were friends."

"And we're not now?" he asked, the question laced with confusion.

"I hardly know you." Granted, that was her fault for pulling away. But how could she not? "To be honest, I don't know if we can go back to being friends."

"You don't mean that … do you?" The hurt in his voice spread to his eyes. He took a step closer to her and she sidestepped, angling herself toward the stairs. "I know things are different between us now, but why can't you give us another chance? Can we at least talk about what happened?"

She shook her head slowly, unable to fully look at him. "I don't think so." She backed toward the stairs. "I'm sorry, Tyler, but … I'm not up to helping you study tonight."

He didn't move. "Slugger." His mouth snapped shut when he caught her glare.

"I *hate* when you call me that." She marched to the door leading out to the side of the house. Opening it, she waved her hand through. "And I need you to leave."

Gemma forced herself not to break down as they eyed each other for a drawn-out moment. Finally, Tyler's posture slipped, and he retrieved his backpack from the floor by his chair. He gave her one last heavy look before stepping out of the house.

Once he'd cleared the threshold, she swung the door shut and flipped the lock. As a fat tear rolled down her cheek, she whirled on her heel and fled up the stairs.

Chapter Nine

Seven Years Earlier

July

Tyler's words echoed in Gemma's head, taunting her: *"It's like I'm losing one of my sisters."* She glanced at her hands bracing against the cool stucco wall on either side of her legs, her mind desperately searching for some way out of this conversation. How could she pretend everything was fine when the boy she'd loved for years thought of her as a sister?

The sound of footsteps approaching saved her from having to respond. *Miracles do exist,* she thought, forcing a smile onto her face.

"Sorry to interrupt," Tyler's mom said. "Ty, I need you to run to the house for a minute and grab that box of Wes's old baby things I set aside for the Laffertys. They're getting ready to leave. It's sitting right by the door."

"Sure, Mom." He nudged Gemma's arm as he swung his legs around to his side of the yard and hopped down. "I'll be right back." Jogging toward the house, he disappeared in the darkness.

Gemma filled her lungs with air, letting it out in a slow breath. *Thank you, Mrs. Abernathy.* Tyler's mom didn't know how perfect her timing was. Now Gemma could make a clean getaway to her room without clueing him in that something was wrong. Not that he'd notice her discomfort anyway. Self-awareness wasn't his strength.

Mrs. Abernathy waited for Gemma to climb down from the wall and walk toward her, then wrapped an arm around her shoulders. "I'll admit, it'll be strange not seeing you two together all the time. You've been such sweet friends for so many years."

Gemma hiccuped a sob, rubbing her nose with the back of her hand.

Mrs. Abernathy stopped walking and turned to face her. "Oh, Gemma. Come here, sweet girl." She cocooned her in a hug.

The sympathy in her tone caused moisture to pool in Gemma's eyes as she held on equally as tight. This woman had become like a second mother to her, a happy casualty of being best friends with her son. Tyler wasn't the only Abernathy she was going to miss.

"You're welcome to come stay with us anytime." Mrs. Abernathy pulled back and placed both her hands on Gemma's cheeks. "Our door is always open, you hear?"

All Gemma could do was nod. She wouldn't be accepting the invitation, but she appreciated it all the same. And she was grateful Mrs. Abernathy didn't try to brush away her emotion, even if she misunderstood the cause of it.

"Thank you," Gemma choked out.

Mrs. Abernathy gave her another hug before they went inside. When Mrs. Carrington pulled Tyler's mom away, Gemma saw that as her chance to escape to her bedroom. She'd had enough socializing for one night.

After changing into her pj's, she crawled underneath her covers. Would Tyler come and find her after he finished his mom's errand? Gemma couldn't deny the tiny morsel of hope that sprouted inside her at the idea. But then annoyance with herself set in. She refused to be desperate. With a huff, she clicked off the light and closed her eyes.

Unfortunately, the loud murmur of conversations from downstairs made falling asleep impossible. Jamming her pillow over her head did little good at blocking out the noise. Where on earth did she put her earplugs?

Groaning in frustration, she tossed the pillow aside and glanced at the clock on her nightstand. The angry neon letters glowed in the darkness, declaring the time as a few minutes after midnight. She frowned. When would all the people leave?

It wasn't uncommon for these parties to go on into the early hours of the morning. But Gemma had never stayed at any of them this late. She couldn't function the next day without the recommended eight hours of sleep, but she was at her best with nine or ten. She wasn't going to get close to any of those numbers tonight. She'd consider herself lucky to get any sleep at all.

And recent circumstances had already proved that luck wasn't on her side.

Finally giving up, she slid out of bed and felt around for her jacket draped over the corner of her dresser. She threw it on, unable to completely push down the disappointment that Tyler hadn't come to find her. *I guess he really does see me as only a sister.* Sighing, she headed back outside, searching for a bit of solace from the suffocating noise happening inside the house.

She wandered along the small patch of grass that ran next to the wall separating her house from the Abernathys. An icy breeze whipped through her, and she shivered. The day hadn't been cold, but once the sun had gone down, the temperature plunged as well. She pulled her jacket tighter around her middle, drawing all the warmth from it she could.

As she rounded the corner of the house, the moon decorated the backyard in silvery light. A dim spotlight shone on the very bench in the far corner she headed toward, as well as the two people sitting on it, in the middle of what looked to be a pretty amazing kiss. Stopping short, she slowly backed up until the house hid her from view.

But curiosity killed the cat, and if Gemma were a feline, she'd most likely be dead because she couldn't resist peeking her head out for another look.

She recognized her twin instantly. The moon reflected off Cassie's golden curls, making her appear like a blonde Aphrodite. Was Aphrodite blonde?

That was something to look up later. Now wasn't the time to analyze the appearance of Greek goddesses.

She leaned forward, attempting to recognize Cassie's latest conquest. The dim lighting made him hard to place, but as her eyes adjusted to the darkness, the very familiar silhouette forced a quiet gasp from her.

Tyler.

No! This couldn't be happening! Gemma's legs felt like she'd fallen into a vat of quicksand. *Move!* she commanded herself, but nothing happened. Shock seized control of her muscles, preventing her from moving even an inch.

Sitting on the wall with Tyler earlier, it hadn't seemed possible for this night to get any worse. It seemed the universe had plans to show her exactly how clueless she was.

No wonder he hadn't come to find her. He'd been too busy.

She rubbed at the ache in her chest, unsure whether to be more heartbroken or angry. Her throat closed up, preventing the scream that attempted to break through as Cassie's slender fingers snaked their way through Tyler's hair and down his shoulders. Tears stung Gemma's eyes, her gaze remaining glued to his hand cradling her sister's waist, tenderly holding her close. She was sure this image would be burned into her memory forever.

Gemma continued to stare at the scene in horror for what seemed like an eternity until he shifted back in his seat. At last, the force cementing her feet to the ground broke. She spun around, teetering slightly off-balance at the sudden burst of motion, and sprinted to the front of the house, her mind racing faster than her feet. Once inside, she snuck up to her room and shut the door.

Discovering Cassie making out with some boy in a dark spot where no one could see wasn't at all surprising. But Tyler? He wasn't the kind of guy who threw around meaningless affection. As far as Gemma knew, he'd never even kissed anyone. Or maybe she'd only been telling herself that because the very idea of it always brought a pain to her heart.

Boy, she'd had no idea just how much it would hurt.

Tyler liked Cassie? How had Gemma missed that? She liked to think she was good at reading his subtle cues. Did she even know him at all?

The emotions crashing over her were too much to carry, and she sank down onto her bed. Curling into a ball beneath her covers, she finally allowed the tears to fall freely down her face.

"This is the worst night of my life," she whimpered through uncontrollable sobs, her face in her pillow to muffle the sound. It didn't take long for the fabric to become drenched. Though whether it was more from her tears or the snot streaming from her nose, she couldn't tell. And she didn't care.

At least he'd be gone in the morning. Gemma couldn't face him again with the picture of that kiss tattooed on her brain. "My life is ruined," she choked out.

And he'd move away having no clue what he'd done to her.

Chapter Ten

Gemma didn't want to be friends?

It was amazing how a single sentence could turn a guy's entire world upside down. Okay, amazing wasn't the right word. Tragic, maybe? That sounded a little too melodramatic. But given Tyler's level of confusion over what Gemma had just said, he had a right to feel dramatic.

He stood on her porch staring at the purple-and-white flower wreath hanging from the door for several long moments after she'd tossed him from the house. Her words tumbled through his mind. He'd thought about her constantly over the last seven years, wondering why she'd never answered his calls. And now that she'd come back into his life again, she didn't even want to try to reignite their friendship? That rejection cut deep.

Brad's going to get a kick out of this, he thought, finally turning from the door and following the path along the side of the house to the front yard. The amount of heckling Tyler had received from his cousin before he'd left was bad enough.

"What part of her are you planning on studying?" Brad had asked as Tyler was walking out the door. "Her eyes or her mouth?"

His cousin could be a little dense when it came to guy-girl relationships. And Tyler could only imagine the amount of roasting he was going to get after less than an hour at Gemma's.

Nope, he knew better than to willingly put himself through that torture.

Tyler got into his car, debating where to go. Maybe his sisters were home. They never seemed to mind when he randomly dropped by.

He had to fight traffic as he drove across town. Some event must have barely ended at the high school, judging by the number of cars streaming from the parking lot. At least the drive to visit Elise and Hallie was a lot shorter than it used to be a few months ago. Their old apartment had been much closer to campus, but the neighborhood left a lot to be desired.

When he pulled into their complex, he located the last available guest space. He grabbed his bag from the passenger seat before walking upstairs to the third floor. Buena Hills was as safe as a Los Angeles suburb could get, and yet, he'd learned the hard way not to leave anything in his car. Almost five years at USC had at least taught him one thing.

Hallie answered the door only seconds after he'd knocked, a pint of her favorite strawberry shortcake ice cream in her hand. "Hey, Ty. Come on in." She moved aside so he could enter.

"Thanks." After stepping into the apartment, he assessed the room.

Elise and Beej claimed opposite sides of the couch underneath the window with similar cartons in their laps. Kendall sat with her legs crossed in one of the worn armchairs in the corner, chowing down on what looked like some kind of chocolate concoction.

"Am I interrupting your girl talk?" he asked, dropping his backpack on the floor.

Hallie plopped down on the second armchair in the opposite corner from Kendall. "Nope, not at all. Elise was telling us all about her day." She gave their sister a conspiratorial look.

Tyler's gaze ping-ponged from Elise—who gave a firm shake of her head—to Hallie, then back to Elise. "What happened?"

Hallie answered before Elise could respond. "Carter proposed today."

"He *what*?" Tyler's protective side clawed its way up his spine. "You're only nineteen!" He realized he was playing into all the big brother stereotypes by going all caveman-like, but that only proved how little he thought of the guy.

"Hallie!" Elise tossed the throw pillow she was leaning on at her younger sister. "I told you he'd freak out."

Tyler struggled a bit not to be offended by that comment. "You said no, right?"

Elise sent an icy stare his way. "Of course I said no. Do you really know me so little as to think I'd marry someone after three dates?"

He breathed a little easier. No, she wouldn't do that. She was way too focused on her dream of seeing the world to throw it away for a loser like Carter.

"It's safe to say he won't be coming around anymore." She patted the middle couch cushion next to her. "Come sit."

Tyler piled a few pieces of paper covered in sketches of what looked like an elaborate cake design and moved them to the edge of the coffee table. Hallie must be planning something special for one of her culinary classes. He squeezed himself in between Elise and Beej on the couch. The girls shimmied a little to make room. "I'm sorry, Elise."

His sister snorted out a laugh. "Don't pretend you're not happy about this. I know you didn't like him." She scooped out a spoonful of mint brownie and pushed it into her mouth.

"You're right. I didn't." He kicked up his legs onto the coffee table, crossing his ankles. "But that doesn't mean I want to see you hurt."

"Trust me. I'm not hurting. I'm more embarrassed than anything." She held out a spoonful of ice cream to him. "Bite?"

Tyler took the spoon and slid it into his mouth. "He actually proposed? Was he that in love with you already?"

She scoffed. "It had nothing to do with love."

"Tell him how he did it," Beej said, unable to contain a giggle. "This is pure gold. I could totally picture it happening in a movie." She nudged Tyler's arm with the back of her hand. "Hey, you want to be a journalist. You should write an article about it and submit it to one of those relationship columns. You could title it *Slow Down Romeo, Proposing Too Soon Gives Off Major Red Flag Vibes*."

"And memorialize my shame forever?" Elise gave a scandalized gasp, though Tyler was relieved she didn't seem too broken up about the experience. "No way. After tonight, we'll never speak of this again."

"Props for the catchy headline, but that kind of journalism sounds miserable," he said to Beej before turning back to Elise. "So, what happened?"

He'd asked the question right as she shoved a large bite of ice cream into her mouth. She squeezed her eyes shut, shuddering a little as she swallowed. "Remember how I'm applying for that semester abroad in Ireland?" she asked after she'd recovered from her brain freeze.

"How can I forget? You've been talking about it nonstop for months."

"Tell me about it," Kendall muttered into her carton.

Elise ignored her. "I turned in my application today."

"Hey, that's great! I bet you're excited." Tyler slugged her thigh gently with his fist.

"Yeah, I am. So excited that I told Carter about it during our lunch date today." She grimaced.

Tyler raised an eyebrow, his suspicions growing about where her story was going. "I take it that didn't go over well?"

"His exact words were"—she stuck her spoon into the carton, holding it between her legs as she used her fingers as air quotes— "'Elise, your priorities are completely mixed up. You need to stay here and look for a husband.'" She shuddered again.

What a chump. If Carter wasn't already out of the picture, Tyler would like to show him how much of a caveman he could be. No one mistreated his sisters.

She scooped her spoon out of the carton again, retrieving a larger bite than any person could comfortably eat. "According to him, good women shouldn't have their own ambitions. They're supposed to marry young and raise lots of babies while supporting their husbands in *their* careers." She shoved the whole bite in her mouth as if the very existence of the creamy mint and chocolate soothed the emotional toll of the whole ordeal.

Kendall made a deep guttural sound of disgust. "What is this, the 1950s? Men are dumb."

"Hey," Tyler objected. "Don't judge us by our worst specimens. We're not all bad."

"No." Kendall smirked, pointing her spoon at him. "Just most of you."

He let the subject drop. There was no convincing her. She'd made her mind up about men long before coming to live with his family. And he'd stopped wondering about what had happened in her childhood to cause her to curse almost every man on the planet. Fortunately, Tyler fell into the small few she found decent.

Or at least tolerated.

"That doesn't sound like a proposal though," he admitted, hoping to get Kendall off her I-hate-men vendetta.

"I haven't gotten to that part yet," Elise said. "After waxing poetic about the role of women, he had the audacity to tell me that he needs a wife to make him look good when he becomes senator. Then he got down on one knee *in the middle of the restaurant* and asked me to marry him."

"How flattering," Tyler said dryly. "How do you even respond to that?"

"I told him that when he finally decides to join the current decade to make sure *not* to call me," she said. "Then I stuck him with the bill and left."

"That's my strong, independent little sis." He gave her a fist bump, then snickered. "You know, I'll be honest. I always thought Beej would be the first one of you to get a random creeper to get down on one knee." His chuckle turned into a full-blown laugh as Beej swung a couch pillow at his head. He brought his hands up in the nick of time to block it.

"Not funny," she said, though a smile still snuck onto her face. It was actually impressive how much his cousin dated. Impressive and not surprising. She was pretty, fun, and loved to flirt. An irresistible combination that made most guys practically fall at her feet.

"Have you seen Gemma at all since last weekend?" Hallie asked.

The sudden change of subject snuffed the smile from his face. "I just came from her house. She was supposed to help me study for my test."

"Yeah?" Elise asked. "That's great you're finally reunited. I know how much you've missed her."

He grunted in response. "I don't think the feeling is mutual."

"What do you mean?" Beej shifted to sit sideways, pulling her legs onto the couch.

How could he explain the situation when he didn't fully understand it himself? He ran a hand over his mouth, replaying the harsh words Gemma had thrown out right before forcing him to leave. But the way she'd said them hadn't been exactly harsh. She'd seemed more sad than angry.

Maybe the girls could help him sort out the meaning behind Gemma's actions. "She invited me over to her house tonight to help me study for my test. Things were going okay during dinner—"

"She made you dinner?" Hallie passed a glance to Beej, who returned it with a significant look of her own.

Tyler often felt like he was on the wrong side of the silent communication with these women. He never understood how the four of them could hold an entire conversation without saying a single word. In this instance, however, he didn't need a PhD to translate what their pointed looks meant. And he had to shut it down.

"It's not like that. I'm pretty sure her grandma made it. It was this whole Christmas dinner-type meal. Gemma seemed kind of embarrassed about the whole thing." His mouth watered remembering the perfectly cooked ham. "It tasted amazing though. The rolls gave yours some tough competition, Hal."

"Can we stay on task, please?" Elise cut in. "What happened next?"

He raised an eyebrow. "You seem extra eager. Do you want me to get you some popcorn?"

She held up her carton with one hand and pointed to it with the other. "I'm good." Then her mouth twitched. "We've already discussed my difficult day. It's only fair for us to move on to yours."

Tyler sighed, still unable to wrap his head around the reason behind Gemma's mood shift. He couldn't even remember what they'd talked about that could have triggered it. "Next thing I knew, she got really closed off and played the whole 'we're practically strangers' card and told me she didn't want to be friends. Then she kicked me out."

Collective gasps passed around the room. He was tempted to laugh at the captive audience but held back.

"Someone get the guy a spoon," Beej called out to no one in particular.

Kendall popped up from her chair and disappeared into the kitchen.

Beej turned to Tyler. "Let the ice cream soothe your soul."

This time, he did laugh. "Is this what you girls do every night? Sit around with ice cream and talk about your problems?"

Kendall reentered the room and handed him a spoon. "It's cheaper than therapy."

In unison, Elise and Beej both held out their cartons to him. He dug his spoon into his cousin's chocolate chip cookie dough.

"You said she pulled away after we moved back to Florida," Hallie said, her rational side taking over the conversation. She'd always been the thinker of the family. The sibling who talked through all her issues to come to the most logical conclusion. "Did you say or do anything to upset her before we left Chile?"

At her question, he swallowed hard, the ice cream freezing his esophagus all the way down as guilt once again lodged in his stomach. He still didn't know what had come over him by letting Cassie kiss him. Had Gemma somehow found out about it?

No, that didn't seem possible. She wasn't there. And he doubted

Cassie would've told her. They weren't the type of sisters to talk about boys.

And besides, even if she did say something about it, why would that matter? There'd been no romantic feelings between him and Gemma. He should be allowed to kiss whoever he wanted. Even if it had been the most embarrassing make-out session he'd ever had. Just thinking about it made him tempted to shudder.

"Tyler?"

He met Hallie's eyes, feeling the weight of her question in uncomfortable ways. How did his sister always seem to know when he was holding something back? She was like Mom in that way.

"I don't know" was all he could come up with.

"Do you even want to still be friends with her?" Kendall asked. "I mean, it's been so long since you've seen her. Maybe you're too different now."

"Of course I do." There was no question. The minute she showed up on his doorstep five days ago, the possibility of not being friends never crossed his mind. They may have grown apart, but that didn't mean they couldn't rebuild some sort of relationship.

"I'm sure she'll come around," Elise said, patting his knee before pushing herself up from the couch. She handed him her ice cream carton. "Here, you can have the rest. I need to study."

Tyler stuck his spoon in the melting dessert and stood as well. "Don't remind me. I still don't know how I'm going to pass my calculus test."

Hallie gave him a sympathetic smile. "I finished everything I have to do for tomorrow. I'll help you."

"Really?" He could've hugged her. And he did, a crushing big brother hug that lifted her off the ground. "You're the best sister ever."

"I heard that!" Elise called from the doorway of her room.

"Thanks for the ice cream. You're both the best."

Walking over to retrieve his backpack, his mind was not on the growing desperation he felt over his looming calculus test. Instead, he unwillingly replayed his final few hours in Chile.

Chapter Eleven

Seven Years Earlier

July

Why am I tasting blood? Tyler thought as something tangy and metallic hit his tongue. He pulled back quickly at the same time that Cassie sucked air through her teeth with a hiss.

Fire engulfed his entire face. He hadn't known what he was expecting his first kiss to be like, but cutting her lip open with his braces wasn't it. "I am *so* sorry!" His voice cracked at the declaration, adding more fuel to the flames of his humiliation.

Cassie pressed the side of her thumb against her mouth. "It's okay," she said, though the way she scooted away from him contradicted her words. She removed her hand, and in the moonlight, he could barely make out a small welt on the fleshy part of her bottom lip. "It happens all the time."

He gave her a doubtful look. "Really?"

"Well, no." She forced out a laugh. "It doesn't. I guess there's a first for everything."

He wasn't even sure how he'd found himself in this position in the first place. One minute, they were joking around about the time he'd ripped the butt of his pants hopping over the chain-link fence at their school, and before he knew it, she was kissing him.

He had to admit he'd occasionally held a passing curiosity about what it would be like to kiss the infamous Cassie Schalk. Maybe it was because of all the times he'd heard about her from the guys at school. It turned out it wasn't as amazing as they'd all made it sound. Lesson learned.

"I'll tell you what," he said, attempting to play it off as if what had just happened wasn't a big deal. "Making out with braces isn't my idea of a good time. That was awkward." His eyes went wide, realizing what he'd implied. "That's not to say that *you* were awkward. Because you weren't. My braces were … awkward." *Stop talking, idiot. You're making it worse.*

Cassie touched his arm. "Really, it's okay. What's a little blood anyway? I have a whole body full of it."

Tyler pressed his back against the bench and stared at the Schalk's house, the lights still glowing merrily inside. The bench they were sitting on was tucked into a far corner of the yard, out of sight of anyone who might have wanted to look out the window. At least that was the hope.

What would people think if they saw him making out with Cassie Schalk the night before he was supposed to be moving away for good? What would Gemma think? He pushed aside the guilt that crept up without warning. She'd probably laugh at him for doing something as pathetic as cutting Cassie's lip open with his braces. He'd rather avoid that embarrassing conversation.

He swiveled slowly to face Cassie, waiting until the last second to meet her eyes. "Do you mind—" How was he supposed to voice this request? "—not telling anyone about this? I can only imagine the texts I'll get from the guys if they find out what happened."

Her lips turned up in a way that Tyler couldn't tell if she pitied him or was being sympathetic. "Sure, no problem."

He gave a brisk nod, then clapped both hands on his thighs before standing. "Well, it's been nice knowing you, Cass."

She stood as well. Tyler hesitated briefly before wrapping an arm around her shoulders in a side hug.

"Have a safe flight tomorrow," she said, reciprocating the friendly gesture. Without another word, she hurried away, her pace betraying how eager she was to get away from him.

The next morning, Tyler stepped out of his bedroom for the last time, pausing for a minute to look back at what used to be his own personal sanctuary. The walls, once covered in posters of his baseball idols, were now bare, the light blue paint chipping where the tape had stuck to it. And the lack of furniture, which had already been shipped back to Florida, caused the shuffle of suitcase wheels on the wooden floor to echo around the room.

He picked up the deflated air mattress he'd slept on all week. Lugging his suitcase behind him, he trudged down the stairs. As he reached the first-floor landing, Mom stepped through the open front door.

"Oh good. You're ready," she said to him before turning to his sisters and Wes sitting on the floor. "Elise, did you do a final walk-through? I saw a few tubes of paint in the upstairs rec room last night."

"I grabbed them." Elise patted her backpack on the floor in front of her. "They're in here."

"I think that's everything, then." Mom gestured to the deflated air mattress tucked underneath Tyler's arm. "We borrowed that one from the Schalks. Will you take it, and the one on the porch, over to them? I'll put your bag in the car."

"Sure, Mom." He wheeled his suitcase over to her. "I want to say goodbye to Gemma anyway." He'd looked for her last night after leaving Cassie, but she'd already gone to sleep.

Mom's mouth puckered down in a sympathetic frown. "Go ahead. But don't take too long." To the rest of the family, she said, "Everyone else, in the car. We have a plane to catch."

Wes practically skipped past Tyler and out the door, no doubt eager to get to the airport to watch the planes take off before their flight. His eight-year-old brother loved everything to do with aviation.

Tyler led his sisters outside, then veered off toward the wall separating their house from the Schalks'. Grunting, he shoved the mattresses over the stucco barrier. He pulled himself up, swinging his legs around to the other side and hopped down onto the grass.

The Schalks' house was quiet. They were probably still sleeping. He yawned, wishing he could've slept a little longer too.

Stepping onto the porch, he dropped his bundle and shook out the strain in his arms. The mattresses weren't too heavy, but the way they were folded made carrying them awkward. He knocked and waited for some sign of life from inside.

Please don't be Cassie. She'd been a good sport about the whole bloody lip thing, but Tyler didn't think he could look her in the eye again for a long, *long* time.

A minute later, the door opened, and he relaxed when Mrs. Schalk appeared, a bathrobe covering her pajama bottoms. She gave him a tired smile, a large coffee mug in her hand. "Good morning, Tyler. I'm surprised to see you on the front porch and not climbing through my daughter's window."

He coughed out a laugh. His climbing habits were no secret to any of Gemma's family members, and they'd never expressed any displeasure with finding him in her bedroom. Still, Mrs. Schalk's no-nonsense-professor look always intimidated him. "I couldn't climb the tree with these in my arms."

"Thank you for bringing them back," she said, morphing into the loving mom he knew she was. "Just set them inside and I'll put them away later."

Tyler heaved the plastic mattresses over the threshold and deposited them out of the way of foot traffic. "Is Gemma awake?" he asked when he'd stood again.

The corners of Mrs. Schalk's mouth turned down in apology. "I'm sorry, Ty. She's not here. She and Cassie walked around the corner to the panadería."

"Oh." His heart sank. She wasn't home? But she knew he was leaving. *Did Cassie tell her about last night?* he thought, discomfort gnawing his stomach at the idea. No, she'd promised she'd keep it to herself. And why would it cause Gemma to avoid seeing him this morning? He didn't do anything wrong.

"Would you tell her I said bye?" he asked Mrs. Schalk, hoping he adequately masked his hurt feelings. "And that I'll call her when I get to Florida?"

"Of course." Her eyes softened even more, and the pity in her expression was almost too much. "We'll miss your family so much. The neighborhood won't be the same without all of you. Travel safe now."

Tyler stood in place for a moment, trying to think up a good reason to stay. If he could prolong his departure a little longer, maybe Gemma would come back before he had to leave.

He came up with nothing.

Finally, he bobbed his head in disappointed resignation. He turned and started walking down the path, barely registering the click of the door as Mrs. Schalk shut it. At the wall, he looked back at Gemma's house again. How could she not wait an extra hour before visiting the panadería? They used to drop in at the corner bakery for chocolate bars a lot on the way home from school. Was a Sahne-Nuss really more important than saying goodbye to her best friend?

Dad was waiting by the open gate when Tyler vaulted back over the wall into the yard.

"All set?" he asked.

"Actually, is it okay if I run over to the panadería for a minute? I'll be quick."

Dad glanced at his watch. "I'm afraid not, son. We're already cutting it close as it is. We don't want to miss our flight."

"Oh." Tyler figured he'd say that, but knowing the answer didn't make hearing it any easier. "Okay."

He turned to get one last look at the house. Six years ago, he'd insisted he could never be happy in this place. Somewhere along the way, Santiago had weaved its way into his heart, and now he didn't want to leave.

"Come on, son," Dad said, reaching past him to put a hand on the iron gate's handle. "Time to go." As he shut the door, the deafening clank closed the book on the Abernathys' life in Chile. He clapped his son on the shoulder. "Maybe you can try out for the team this year at your new school."

Tyler only managed a half-hearted smile. He knew what Dad was doing, and he appreciated the attempt at distracting them both from the heavy emotions. On the one hand, they were going home, back to their family roots. And yet, it didn't feel like it.

"Yeah, I think I'll do that," he said, taking the bait anyway.

But questions over Gemma's behavior crowded out any thoughts of baseball as he slid into the backseat next to Hallie. He didn't even get to say goodbye. What if he never saw her again?

Chapter Twelve

Time healed all wounds.

Wasn't that what people always said? Gemma had tattooed those words on her heart the day Tyler left Santiago. And she'd started repeating them to herself again two days ago after she'd dropped the whole I-don't-want-to-be-friends bombshell on him. What had she learned from it all?

People were fools.

Time heals all wounds? What a load of garbage. Or maybe there was something wrong with her.

That had to be the only explanation for why she felt so bad about the things she'd said. But what was she supposed to do? Tyler had backed her into a corner—metaphorically, not physically, thank goodness—forcing her brain into fight-or-flight mode. She'd tossed out the one thing she knew would disarm him.

There was no coming back from that. Which was her intention all along, right? So why was the guilt still eating away at her?

"Is everything alright, dear?" Gram asked during lunch on Friday, pulling Gemma from her guilt-induced spiraling. "Your thoughts seem far away. And you've hardly touched your food."

Gemma needed to work on her poker face. "I guess I'm a little tired." Who wouldn't be with the picture of Tyler's hurt face ready to greet her whenever she closed her eyes? The guy would not go away.

Gram's brows turned down in concern as she studied her granddaughter, her fork hovering near her pursed mouth. "You really should eat something. This alfredo is delicious. Thank you for making it."

"It wasn't a big thing. I'm happy to help." Gemma speared a small piece of broccoli and popped it in her mouth to appease her grandmother. "You've seemed more tired the last couple days as well. Have you been sleeping okay?"

"No worse than usual," Gram admitted, laying her fork across her empty plate.

The dark circles under her eyes did little to convince Gemma of that. But her grandmother refused to admit to anyone that she wasn't as fit as the fiddle she used to be.

"It's been so wonderful having you here. I've been so lonely since your grandpa ... left." Unmistakable longing entered Gram's green eyes. She rarely referred to Grandpa Will's death, preferring to think of the happy times with him. "That man used to drive me up the wall, but no one made me laugh as hard as he did. I could never stay mad at him."

Gemma smiled as one of her favorite memories of her grandfather resurfaced in her mind. He'd always had crisp twenty-dollar bills waiting for her and Cassie whenever they came to visit. Mom had blown a gasket one day when she'd discovered him teaching them how to use that money to play poker when they were eleven. Gemma wasn't sure what had been said to him, but after that day, the only betting "money" they could use were jellybeans.

"I miss him," she said, reaching over to squeeze Gram's hand. The skin felt soft and paper-thin underneath Gemma's palm.

"Me too." Sadness tainted Gram's whisper.

Gemma knew her grandparents weren't perfect. Still, it was hard not to put their marriage on a pedestal. They'd loved each other so fiercely, and it was only natural for that love to trickle down to everyone who came into their circle of influence. Her future husband had some impossible shoes to fill. Maybe that was why Blake hadn't worked out.

Against her will, her thoughts drifted to Tyler, and her stomach bubbled uncomfortably. She most definitely wouldn't find what she was looking for with him.

"Look at us getting all sentimental. Grandpa wouldn't want us to sit around and be sad." Gram bobbed her head with finality. "Let's get lunch cleaned up. What time is your interview?"

"Not until four."

Gemma had been a little hesitant about getting a job when she'd first arrived in Buena Hills. What if something happened to Gram while she was away from the house? What if she fell and hurt herself? The very idea made Gemma think twice about ever leaving.

"I know how to use a phone like a normal person," Gram had said when Gemma voiced her concerns out loud. "You shouldn't stick around here like a hermit. You're young. Get out and experience the world." She'd said it with a smile, but the forceful way the words had emerged had spoken of frustration. It couldn't be easy being faced with the reality that tasks she once did with ease weren't as simple anymore.

And besides, Gemma wouldn't be able to hover over Gram once school started in the fall anyway. She might as well get used to the constant worry.

"You should give Tyler a call," Gram said at the same time Gemma lifted her cup to her mouth. "I'm sure he'd like to see you again."

Water shot from Gemma's mouth, drenching everything in its path. She sputtered out a cough to clear the liquid from her trachea, still getting over the shock of her grandmother's sudden suggestion.

Gram thumped her on the back.

"Why would I do that?" Gemma wheezed as soon as she could speak. Grabbing the napkin next to her plate, she dabbed at the water dribbling down her chin.

Gram continued rubbing circles around Gemma's back. "I'm smart enough to see that something happened between you two that makes you uncomfortable around him. I just can't figure out what it could be. And judging by the way Tyler has responded to you, I don't think he knows either."

"He doesn't." Gemma could admit that much. "And he can't know. It's not something I can talk about with him." Confessing that she was bothered by the kiss he'd shared with Cassie would also require Gemma to fess up to her true feelings for him. She couldn't cope with the heartbreak of having him reject her again. Besides, he wasn't even supposed to know she'd seen them. She'd prefer to keep it that way.

"Are you sure about that? He seems like a nice one. I'd think he'd at least try to understand. I, for one, wouldn't mind having that fine man hanging around the house a little more. And that tush!" Gram fanned her face with her hand. "Whoooeeee!"

"*Grandma.*"

"What?" Gram asked, her mouth morphing into a sly smile. "I might be old, but my eyesight is still sharp as a hawk's, thank you kindly."

"Even so, you shouldn't be talking about Tyler's"—Gemma dropped her voice to a hiss while her gaze flitted around the room, then back to Gram—"tush." She wasn't sure why she felt the need to whisper. It wasn't like he was nearby. And yet, the mention of Tyler's backside, however nice it might be—and it was pretty nice, if she were being honest—made her want to crawl into a hole and stay there forever. "He's not a piece of meat."

Gram shrugged. "Appreciating beauty is one of the pleasures of life. Don't rob me of that."

Gemma sputtered out a laugh. Her grandma's feisty personality was one of her favorite things about the woman.

"I'll clean up lunch." She pushed back from the table. "Why don't you go upstairs and rest?"

"Are you just trying to get rid of me so you can stop blushing?"

"No, of course not," Gemma said hastily, then grabbed their plates and walked over to the sink. Because they needed to be cleaned, of course. Not because she didn't want Gram to see that she actually was blushing.

Gram laughed. "Don't try to hide it from me. I wasn't born yesterday." But she took pity on her granddaughter. "I do have a headache though. I think I'll go lie down for a while." She rose from her chair, wobbling a little before catching herself with a hand on the table.

Unease pricked at Gemma's heart as she watched her grandma stand motionless, attempting to steady herself. "Are you okay, Gram?"

"Stood up too fast, I suppose." Gram began a slow shuffle to the stairs.

Something wasn't right. Her grandma's steps were growing more unsteady the farther she got from the table. True, Gram wasn't as mobile as she used to be, but she'd never had trouble moving around the house.

"Why don't I help you up to your room?" Gemma said, taking a hesitant step forward, her hands still gripping the plates.

"I'm only a little dizzy, dear." Gram shuffled another harrowing step toward the stairs, then stopped and swayed.

Stubbornness aside, Gemma couldn't let her grandma continue without support. With her uneasiness growing into fear, she set the plates in the sink and hurried over.

But seconds before she reached her, Gram lost the battle with her balance and went down hard. A sickening crunch rang through the kitchen, followed by a cry of pain.

"Gram!" Gemma kneeled on the floor next to her grandmother and took her uninjured hand, peering into her face. What she saw there snapped the razor-thin thread keeping what was left of Gemma's calm intact.

Gram's unfocused gaze stared back, contorted with confusion. One side of her mouth opened a crack as if she were trying to speak. Only the left side. The right drooped a little, and the unsettling sight sent icy prickles of dread down Gemma's spine.

"We need to get you to the hospital," she said through her clenched jaw. She wouldn't cry, even though the weight of responsibility bore down on her like Atlas with the world on his back. She had to keep it together for both their sakes.

She eyed her phone charging on the far counter, way out of her reach. What was she supposed to do? She didn't want to abandon Gram's side, but she couldn't leave her on the floor like this. What if she did more damage than good by moving her?

Now wasn't the time for indecision. She had to act. Placing her free hand on Gram's back, she very carefully lifted her into a sitting position. Gram cried out in pain, and a tear trailed down Gemma's cheek in response. She brushed it away before helping her grandmother shuffle a few inches to lean her back against the wall.

"I'll be right back." Gemma dashed to the far side of the kitchen, snatching her phone off the counter with a force that yanked the charger from the wall. With trembling fingers, she dialed 911.

Chapter Thirteen

"Your grandmother has experienced a stroke."

Gemma's heart plummeted to her stomach as the paramedic confirmed what she'd already suspected. Standing on her front porch, she kept her eyes glued to the welcome mat at her feet to keep them from straying to the two EMTs pushing Gram's stretcher into the waiting ambulance. She couldn't look at it. Not if she wanted to stay strong. And she needed to stay strong. She couldn't break down now.

"Will she be ..." The words caught in her throat as she finally looked up at him, fear gripping every inch of her body at the possibility that her beloved grandmother might not be okay.

The paramedic hooked his fingers through the belt loops of his navy cargo pants. His brown eyes watched her with compassion from underneath thick, graying eyebrows. "We're going to do everything we can to assure your grandmother has the best care possible. You did a good thing getting her help so early. We'd appreciate if you'd come in the ambulance in case we need to ask you for additional information. Would that be alright?"

She nodded. "Of course."

He gestured for her to follow him and got her situated in the back next to the stretcher. Gemma flinched at the deafening clank of metal that echoed through the confined space as the paramedic closed the door.

She took her grandmother's hand gently. "It's going to be okay, Gram," she said, trying to reassure herself as well.

Gram didn't respond. Gemma wasn't sure if her grandmother was even capable of saying anything.

The ride wasn't long—ten minutes? maybe less?—but it seemed

like a lifetime passed before they pulled into the back of the emergency room at the Buena Hills hospital. She didn't let go of Gram's hand the whole way, willing for a positive outcome to this terrifying situation.

What would happen now? Would Gram recover? *She has to,* Gemma thought desperately.

One thing was for certain. She needed to tell her parents. Cassie would want to know what happened too. When the ambulance stopped in front of the automatic doors of the emergency room, Gemma watched the paramedics wheel the stretcher into the building. As much as she didn't want to leave her grandmother's side, there wasn't anything she could do for her now that she was in the care of medical professionals.

After checking in at the reception desk, she went searching for a quiet place to call her parents. A chill crept over her as she followed the artificially bright hallway away from the ER. She hadn't been in many hospitals, and the few times she had, it always surprised her that they weren't bustling with activity like she saw on TV. In fact, she didn't see a single soul anywhere. The hospital was quiet today. That should be a good thing, although it only served to make her feel more alone.

When she reached a fork in her path, Gemma glanced at the signs hanging down from the ceiling above her. The cardiology and radiology wings veered off to her left. Up ahead, an arrow pointed out labor and delivery to her right. She kept walking straight, keeping her breaths steady, even as her thoughts swirled with uncertainty.

Her foot caught on the floor, and she stumbled a bit, noticing that the squeaky-clean tile of the medical areas had met a carpeted ramp leading down to the hospital's main lobby.

Sunlight streamed through the skylights, hitting the atrium that took up the entire wall across from the revolving entrance. The sound of water trickling from the fountain below the plants echoed off the high-vaulted ceiling, providing a surprising amount of relief to her rising panic.

Pulling her phone from her back pocket, she typed out a quick text to Cassie.

> Gemma: Gram had a stroke. Call me ASAP.

She felt bad for the abruptness and lack of details, but she knew her sister would pick up on the urgency of the situation. Finding an empty armchair near the atrium, she waited a full minute for some kind of response. Nothing. Trusting that Cassie would call when she saw the text, Gemma dialed Dad.

He must be in a meeting, she thought when it went straight to voicemail. She knew that he often turned his phone off when consulting with important clients. She also knew that he sometimes forgot to turn it back on afterward.

Thankfully, Mom picked up quickly. Gemma tried to keep her voice steady as she launched into the details of what happened in the kitchen and what she'd learned from the paramedics.

"Oh sweetie," Mom said. "I'm so sorry you had to handle this on your own. This is why I had my doubts when you said you wanted to move in with Gram. I was worried something like this would happen."

"No, don't be sorry. You couldn't have known. Gram's getting older, but she was still pretty healthy before now." Gemma rose from her chair, her uncertainty and fear making it impossible to sit still. She began pacing the length of the atrium. How would Gram's quality of life be affected after today? Would she even be able to live in the home she refused to leave, her strongest connection to her departed husband?

Mom cleared her throat. "Still, I hate that you're alone over there, dealing with this by yourself. Have you told your father?"

"I tried calling him, but he didn't answer."

"Hm," Mom hummed into the phone. "I know he had a meeting

this afternoon. Let me tell him. We'll work on arranging our schedules and figuring out flights so we can come down as soon as possible."

"Okay." Gemma reached the end of the atrium and turned slowly on her heel, starting back the way she'd come. She felt bad at the prospect of her parents dropping everything to come down to California right now. Dad was right in the middle of tax season, and Mom's classes at the university didn't end for several more weeks. Gemma had willingly volunteered to help Gram, and that's what she intended to do. But she couldn't deny that she needed her parents right now.

"Don't feel bad," Mom insisted when Gemma expressed her concerns out loud. "This isn't something you should have to handle on your own. I'll get a hold of your father and start working it out with my TAs. I'm sure I can arrange for them to teach my classes, at least until we figure out what kind of care Gram will need. Will you call me as soon as you have an update?"

"Yes." The word cracked, and Gemma cleared her throat. "Thanks, Mom."

She ended the call. Her phone screen didn't have a chance to go dark before it buzzed with a call from Cassie.

"Gram had a stroke?" she asked before Gemma had even said hello. "When?"

Cassie's frantic energy did little to help Gemma's rising worry. Her pacing picked up speed as she repeated the information she'd already told Mom.

"Is she going to be okay?" her sister asked. "What's going to happen to her?"

Gemma blew out a loaded breath. "I don't know. No one's told me anything." She heard voices in the background on the other end of the line and wondered if her sister had ducked out of work to make the call.

"Hang on." A muffled conversation then took place while Gemma waited for Cassie to come back on the line. "Gem?" A hint of annoyance was evident in that one syllable. "I have to go. But call me as soon as you know how Gram is. I'll have my phone with me all afternoon."

"I will. I promise."

And then Cassie was gone. Gemma pocketed her phone and meandered back through the hallways until she found the ER's waiting room. The dimly lit space was much different than the peaceful lobby, or even the brightly lit hallways of the rest of the hospital, but it matched the gloomy aura of the stony-faced people waiting for news of their loved ones. She sat down near a large potted ficus, a few seats away from a young mom bouncing her crying toddler while pressing an ice pack to his forehead.

Drumming the fingers of one hand against her leg, Gemma pulled out her phone again and opened the e-book she'd started yesterday. But after reading the same paragraph three times and still not internalizing what was happening in the story, she dropped the device between her thighs and sighed.

What if Gram didn't recover? Tears stung Gemma's eyes at the possibility. Her grandma had been one of her favorite people her whole life, the person she looked forward to visiting every summer as a kid. The woman who loved her and cherished her as much as her own mom did. The woman who stocked her freezer full of home-made bread, and who made Christmas dinner in July, and always gave the best hugs. Gemma couldn't bear the thought of losing her.

The hum of quiet conversations buzzed around her, but she didn't bother attempting to make out what was being said. Any time the doors to the ER opened, her gaze jumped to them, willing it to be someone who could tell her what was going on. But as the minutes ticked past, Gemma waited, her anxiety growing too much for her to bear.

How long had it been? Ten minutes? Twenty? Gemma couldn't recall when they'd arrived at the hospital in the first place. It was sometime after one. She glanced at the digital clock hanging on the opposite wall. The black numbers displayed the time as five minutes to two.

If only there was someone she could call. She pulled out her phone again and scrolled through her contact list. Before she moved down to California, she wouldn't have hesitated to call any of her roommates. They'd always had each other's backs during moments of need. Blake had also been a proven confidant, even after they'd broken up for the last time.

But none of them were in the same state, and Gemma didn't need another phone conversation. What she craved was the real, tangible comfort of having someone here next to her. Her finger stopped scrolling and hovered over one name.

Tyler.

She'd saved him in her contacts under just his first name after they'd exchanged numbers when she'd invited him over to study. The reminder of their falling out only added to the sick feeling growing in the pit of her stomach. There was a time when he'd have been the first person she called about anything. But she couldn't reach out to him now. Not after the things she said the other night.

On the other hand, was she really up to the emotional burden of waiting alone?

Chapter Fourteen

Tyler leaned back in his chair and stretched, but the crick remained in the center of his spine. Even with the padding, the structure of the seats in this lecture hall always hit his back in the worst possible spot. He wouldn't be surprised if whoever had constructed this building intentionally found the most uncomfortable seats to make it impossible to fall asleep during class.

The chairs were the least of his problems once his phone started vibrating in his pocket though. Professor James detested any kind of interruptions during his lectures. He'd already called out one of his students at the beginning of class for a chirping mobile.

Without pulling the device from his pocket, Tyler squeezed the sides of it through his jeans to silence the hum and refocused on Professor James's lesson on Mayan history. He tapped a few notes into the Word document open on the laptop resting on his thighs. With his long legs, the little desks attached to the chair were never worth using.

A minute later, more buzzing tickled his leg. He could practically feel the glare from the woman sitting next to him. After shooting an apologetic glance her way, he pulled the cell from his pocket and stared at the screen as the number flashed back at him.

Gemma?

He hadn't heard from her since she'd kicked him out of her house two days ago. What more could she possibly have to say to him? She'd made it very clear she didn't want to be friends.

Tyler glanced at the clock on the wall to his right. Twenty-three minutes until the end of class. Whatever she had to say would have to wait. She couldn't expect him to drop everything for her. Even if he always had in the past. And was tempted to now, if he were being honest. He buried his phone back into his pocket.

When it went off a third time, he didn't only feel the annoyance of the girl next to him, he heard it as well. Her groan was quiet but intense.

"Sorry," he whispered.

She narrowed her eyes at him briefly before raising her chin and turning back to the front.

Reluctantly, he pulled his phone out again and was greeted by Gemma's name on the screen a second time. Something cinched up in Tyler's stomach. She wasn't the needy type. Whatever the reason for her call, it must be important.

After making sure his notes were saved, he shut his laptop and slid it into his bag. Then he looked down his row to the right. Several people filled the seats between himself and the end. He shifted to glance to his left. The same scenario met him in that direction as well. But the woman to his right was already annoyed enough with him so he decided to take his chances with his classmates to the left.

He executed a weird little twisting maneuver to slide his bag onto his back before he half stood. "Excuse me," he whispered to the guy next to him, who sat up straighter and attempted to move his legs to the side. Tyler crawled over him as discreetly as he could.

"Excuse me," he repeated softly to the next person. And again, as he maneuvered his way through the row to the exit. His fellow students, some of whom had taken advantage of the padded seats to catch up on some much-needed snoozing, grumbled quietly at the disruption. Apparently, the chairs weren't horrible for everyone.

"Is what I have to teach not entertaining enough for you, Mr. Abernathy?" Professor James asked from the front of the classroom.

Tyler froze, half crouching, half crawling over a particularly long-legged woman occupying the last seat in the row. *So close,* he thought, slowly swiveling to meet his professor's hard stare. "Uh, it's an emergency." His face burned, and he refused to meet the woman's eye as he hopped over her and scurried from the lecture hall before Professor James could say anything more.

By the time Tyler reached the hallway and the door clicked shut behind him, the buzzing had stopped. He unlocked his phone to return Gemma's call, but she beat him to it.

Leaning his hip against the wall, he lifted the phone to his ear. "Hey, Slu—" He cleared his throat. Old habits were hard to break. "What's up?"

"Oh Tyler, thank goodness you answered."

Tension seized his body at the distress in her voice. "What's wrong?"

A long strain of panicked rambling followed. Tyler only made out a word here and there, not enough to grasp the whole message.

"Whoa, whoa. Slow down. I don't understand what you're saying." Dropping his head, he plugged his other ear, attempting to block out the conversation of a group of students nearby.

Gemma took in a shaky breath. "It's my grandma. She ... had a stroke." She squeaked out a sob. "The doctors are running some tests, but no one has come out to tell me anything. I'm so scared."

Tyler's heart sank. Poor Gem. Grandma June meant everything to her. Every ounce of petty hurt lingering from the other night drained from his body. "Where are you?"

"The emergency room in Buena Hills."

He pushed off the wall and started walking. "Hold tight, Gem. I'll be there as soon as I can."

Tyler rushed through the doors of the emergency room, cursing the Southern California traffic. He scanned the waiting area for any sign of Gemma, puffing out a huge breath of relief when she rushed over to him, launching into his outstretched arms. Wrapping his protective shield around her, he held her close as she sobbed against his chest.

"I'm here," he said. The words seemed insufficient, but what else could he say to her right now? She was never the type to find comfort in empty reassurances.

He continued to hold her, rubbing soft circles along her back, aware of the not-so-discreet glances being cast their way by the other people in the room. Tyler paid them no heed, though it was harder to ignore the pounding of his heart that had picked up the second Gemma stepped into his arms. He was just concerned over her well-being, of course.

It took some time for her to regain her composure. When her sobs gradually stilled, she stepped back, dabbing her wet cheekbones with the backs of her thumbs. Mascara smudged under her eyes, and Tyler brushed it away with his fingertips.

"Thank you," she said with an embarrassed laugh.

He shrugged her comment away. "Tell me what happened." Snagging her hand, he ignored the zing traveling up his arm. Now was not the time to contemplate the meaning behind that sensation. He led her to a set of chairs along the back wall of the waiting room, next to the large ficus. From where they sat, they'd have a good view of the doors leading back to the ER so Gemma would know as soon as the doctor came out with news.

She continued to swipe at her eyes with her free hand. "Gram was really tired after lunch today, so she decided to lie down for a while. She fell on her way to the stairs. But when I got to her, it was the look in her eyes that really terrified me. Like she had no idea where she was." She gasped out a sob. "The paramedics brought us here. I wasn't sure what to do after I talked to my family. I'm sorry to bother you, I didn't know who else to call."

"Never be sorry for calling me." He meant it. No amount of hurtful words could ever turn him away when she needed help. Had they really fallen so far from where they were as kids that she didn't know that?

She lifted her shoulders to her ears before letting them drop. "I thought after what I said to you ..."

"Why *did* you say those things?" The question slipped out before he could stop it. "Ever since you came to my house last week, you've seemed like you want nothing to do with me. Why?"

She wrapped her arms around her middle. "It just felt like you expected us to be best friends like we were in Chile. But we're not kids anymore. We haven't seen each other for seven years. Everything has changed."

Tyler didn't think he'd changed that much, though it seemed that she certainly had. "Believe it or not, I actually don't expect it to be exactly the way it was before. But that doesn't mean I don't want to *try*. I still care about you, and I always will, no matter how many years pass or how much we've both changed."

Gemma kept her gaze on the scuffed-up gray tile at their feet. "I don't know what to think about it all. I'm kind of going through some things right now."

When she finally lifted her head, fresh tears pooled in her hazel eyes. A stab of guilt pricked his stomach. Now wasn't the best time to hash out this argument. Not with her already in such an emotional state over Grandma June. He held back any further line of questioning.

"I know." He reached over to wipe another smudge of mascara off her cheek. "How can I help?"

At that, some of the rigidity in her shoulders lifted, and she aimed the tiniest of smiles in his direction. "I'm not alone. That helps. I hope I didn't interrupt anything important."

Tyler bumped her arm with his elbow. "There's nothing more important than being here for you when you need it."

She cocked her head to the side as she studied him, a very clear question in her eyes. Was it really so hard for her to trust that he was being honest with her?

At the sound of doors whooshing open, Gemma jerked her head

in the direction of the emergency room. A nurse in light blue scrubs walked out, heading for the triage area.

Gemma slumped back in her seat with a heavy sigh. "Man, I wish someone would tell me what's going on." She shook her hands out at her sides, a nervous tick Tyler remembered well from their childhood.

"How long have you been waiting?"

Gemma glanced at the digital clock on the wall across from them. "Almost two hours. The nurse said they needed to run some tests. I don't know how long they're supposed to take." She bolted upright before turning quickly toward him again. "Tyler, what if she doesn't make it? I already lost my grandpa. I can't lose Gram too."

"Hey, we don't know anything yet. Let's wait until we figure out what's happening before jumping to conclusions." He grabbed her shaking hand, interlocking their fingers and resting them between their thighs.

Gemma took a deep breath in and released it slowly. "You're right. There's no use making more out of the situation before learning the facts."

Their physical connection seemed to have a calming effect on her, judging by how her grip softened in his and the way she relaxed back into her chair. Tyler was glad for it because holding her hand had the opposite effect on him.

They'd sat this way countless times as kids whenever one of them needed comfort or during intense movies, even though neither of them was willing to admit they were scared. And sometimes, simply because they wanted to. But not once during any of those instances had holding her hand made his heart race so fast it rivaled a horse galloping toward the finish line of the Kentucky Derby.

Beside him, Gemma sighed again. "It's just so hard not to worry."

"I get that," he said, pulling his focus off the unsettling feeling.

Slowly, she swiveled toward him and studied his face. What was she searching for? Her uncertainty made him want to wrap her up in his arms and shield her from all her problems. Finally, her mouth twitched ever so slightly before relaxing again. Was that a smile?

"Thank you for being here with me. I think the wait would be far more excruciating being alone." And then she did something he never would've expected. She leaned her head on his shoulder.

He tensed, though his insides buzzed like a million bumblebees crammed inside his six-foot frame. "I'd go anywhere in the world for you," he whispered, resting his temple on her hair.

They sat in silence for a few moments while the low murmur of conversation from those mulling about the waiting room mixed with the purr of the AC. Somewhere in the hospital, a voice came over the intercom calling for a Dr. Thompson to report to labor and delivery.

Gemma's head on his shoulder made it impossible for Tyler to relax. The sweet scent of her dark curls intoxicated his senses. Hmm. He didn't remember her smelling this good when they were kids. And how was he supposed to get his heart to slow down? It couldn't be healthy for his pulse to be this elevated for so long while his body was at rest. Maybe he should check himself into triage while he was here.

He searched for something to distract him from the confusing emotions seizing control of him, his mouth lifting as a memory popped into his head. "Do you remember the last time we were in the hospital together?"

Her head shook slightly against his shoulder as she chuckled softly. "We were thirteen. I still can't believe you talked me into riding that sketchy, wheeled toboggan you and Max Henley built. I knew something bad would happen just looking at it." She sat up and threw an exasperated look at him.

"Hey, that toboggan was amazing. It was my aim you had to worry about," Tyler said in a self-deprecating way. "I had no doubt I'd be able to steer us through the gap in that cement wall."

"I knew my arm was broken the minute we ran into it." Gemma giggled. At least she could laugh about it now. "I was so mad at you.

The only consolation was that you broke yours too. But I still swore I'd never talk to you again."

Thankfully, her threat had only lasted about four hours. The longest four hours of his life up to that point. "Even after you ended your silent treatment, you still sullied my cast with 'Tyler is a moron' in bright pink Sharpie for everyone to see."

"Of course," she said simply. "Just because I was speaking to you, didn't mean I'd forgiven you."

Tyler laughed. "We had a lot of good times back then, didn't we?"

A soft smile appeared on her face at that. "Yeah, we did."

He studied the grown-up version of his best friend, his pulse picking up again. "I've really missed you, Gem."

Her hazel eyes narrowed in question before her gaze dropped to their ball of hands still resting between their thighs. Had she just realized their fingers were still tangled together? It was so natural, and yet ... different.

"I've missed you too."

After so much reluctance to even be near him over the last week, her admission was huge. He had no response to it. And even if he did, he didn't have the chance to give it. The doors to the emergency room opened again, claiming Gemma's attention immediately. Her head swiveled, and she looked expectantly at a woman in navy scrubs who stepped into the waiting room, consulting her clipboard. "Ms. Schalk?"

Gemma popped up from her seat and rushed to her. "Yes, that's me."

Tyler followed, stopping a step behind her. The woman acknowledged him with a brief nod of her head before addressing Gemma. "I'm Dr. Fields. I'm one of the neurosurgeons here at the hospital. I've run some initial tests on your grandmother. An MRI on her brain has shown a blood clot in the cerebellum region, which is what caused her stroke."

Gemma's breath caught. "Is she going to be okay?" Her hand shot behind her, searching for Tyler. He latched on, more than happy to be her source of strength during this difficult conversation.

"It's too soon to determine how her recovery will go," Dr. Fields responded. "But I will say that it's encouraging that her stroke was caused by a blood clot and not a more serious condition. The fact that she's in relatively good health overall is also a good sign."

Gemma's grip on Tyler's hand loosened a tiny bit. "What happens now?"

Dr. Fields was the perfect picture of a compassionate doctor. "We've transferred her to the stroke center here at the hospital and have started her on a medication that will help dissolve the clot and improve blood flow to her brain. We'd like to keep her here for the time being to monitor her vital signs and develop her care plan until we feel she's in the clear to go home."

"What about her arm?" Gemma asked. "She seemed in a lot of pain during the ambulance ride."

Dr. Fields bobbed her head. "She has a slight fracture in her ulna near the elbow, which has been stabilized for now while we're addressing her stroke. Fortunately, the orthopedist has informed me that the break isn't severe enough to require surgery. But I'll allow him to give you more details on treatment for it."

Gemma let out a breath. "When can I see her?"

"She'll be available for visitors in a few minutes." Dr. Fields indicated the waiting room exit that led to the main hospital lobby. "When you're ready, go out through those doors and around the corner. Laura, at the information desk, can direct you to the stroke center. Someone will be waiting to give you a visitor's pass and show you to your grandmother's room once she's settled."

"Thank you," Gemma said, nodding her understanding.

Dr. Fields smiled. "Of course. And if you have any questions at all, please don't hesitate to ask."

Gemma thanked her again. Dr. Fields parted with another nod before retreating through the same doors she'd come out of moments ago.

Once they were alone again, Tyler gently turned Gemma to face him. Her brows scrunched together in worry, and a large tear hovered on the end of her lashes.

"Come here." He pulled her into his arms. "You look like you could use a hug."

She sagged in his embrace as if she didn't have the strength to stand on her own legs anymore. After a brief pause, her arms came around his middle to rest on his back. "I should probably call my parents," she said, not lifting her cheek from his chest. "And Cassie. They'll want an update."

Tyler pushed her back slightly, keeping his hands on both her arms as he searched her face. "Would it help if I called your family? I'm sure you're anxious to be with your grandma."

She considered him for a drawn-out minute. "No, that's okay. I should be the one to call them. I mean, you haven't talked to them in years." Her eyebrows drew together like she was unsure about something. "You haven't, right?"

"No," he admitted. "But I really don't mind if it would help you out."

"Are you sure?" she asked, tangling her fingers in a ball in front of her. "Wouldn't it be strange for you, calling some people you haven't seen in years?"

Tyler couldn't resist a little chuckle as he dropped his head. "No, it wouldn't. Don't worry about me. I just want to help." He pulled his phone from his back pocket and unlocked the screen before holding it out to her. "What's your dad's number?"

Gemma visibly relaxed as she took it and typed in the number in a new contact. "Thank you, Tyler. Will you tell him that I'll call when I can?"

"Yes." He took the phone back from her. "What's Cassie's number? I'll send her a text too."

Gemma's shoulders tensed briefly at the mention of Cassie, but she tilted her head as she studied him for a few seconds. Then all tension seemed to vanish from her body, and she looked relieved.

Wait, what?

"I'll text it to you," she said.

As she toggled through her contacts, Tyler had a hard time ignoring the unsettling feeling swirling around in his gut. She'd reacted strangely when they'd talked about Cassie during dinner the other night. If he remembered correctly, that very conversation had led to the abrupt end to the evening. Was something going on in their relationship? Or was there more to it? *Had* Cassie mentioned the kiss? Why did the idea of Gemma finding out about it bother him so much? Should he bring it up?

No. Now wasn't the time. He nudged her shoulder instead. "Give my best to Grandma June. I'll take care of things out here."

Gemma weaved their fingers together and squeezed his hand. "Thank you," she said again. Then she stepped past him and continued toward the exit. He watched her go, worry over Grandma June warring with unease over Gemma's reaction to his offer to call her family. And mixed with it all was the confusing way his body responded every time she was nearby.

He had no idea what to do about that.

Chapter Fifteen

"Knock, knock."

At the familiar voice, Gemma glanced up from the book in her lap to the doorway of Gram's hospital room.

Tyler stood there, a large bouquet of yellow roses and white daisies blocking one side of his face. She hadn't seen him since the day before when she'd left him in the ER lobby. And even though he'd texted her to ask if he could stop by, her stomach still flipped a little at the sight of him.

"May I come in?" he asked, hovering half in, half out of the room.

She bit down on a smile and turned her attention to the bed across the room, leaving the decision up to Gram. Nurse Sadie's position in front of her bed blocked most of her from view. All Gemma could see was Gram's hand as it snaked out from underneath the thin hospital blanket, waving weakly for Tyler to come inside.

"Did you come to visit me, boy?" Her voice was raspy, and she spoke slowly, slurring her words a little.

"I wanted to check in on you," he said as he stepped up to the foot of her bed. A twinkle appeared in his eye. "I heard you took a little spill yesterday."

Gram chuckled softly, and the sound lifted some of the worry still gripping Gemma's heart. Her grandmother had always had a sharp sense of humor. It was encouraging to hear even a weak laugh from her.

"What beautiful flowers," Sadie said in a tone as cheerful as the yellow in the bouquet. She draped her stethoscope loosely over the back of her neck.

Tyler assessed the blooms in his arms. "My mom always told me never to visit someone in the hospital empty-handed."

"She's a smart woman," the nurse said through a laugh, unwrapping the blood pressure cuff from Gram's thin bicep. She placed a light hand on her patient's shoulder. "I'm all done here. I'll come check on you a little later, okay?"

Gram gave her a weak smile as she held out a shaking hand. Sadie took it briefly before stepping away to gather her equipment.

A few different nurses had come in to check on Gram in the last twenty-four hours, but Sadie's compassionate bedside manner had quickly made her Gemma's favorite. The woman was a perfect fit for a career in healthcare.

"Why don't I go see if I can find a vase to put these in?" Sadie relieved Tyler of his bundle and left the room.

Once she was gone, Gemma reclaimed the chair next to Gram's bed that she'd abandoned to be out of the way during Sadie's checks.

Tyler approached the other side and, without hesitating, bent to kiss Gram's wrinkled cheek. "It's good to see you, Grandma June. You look like a million bucks."

Gram lightly batted his hand that rested on the mattress next to her. "Gemma never mentioned … you were such a t-tease."

"No teasing. Cross my heart." He pulled a chair up to the bed and sat. "How are you feeling though? Can I do anything for you?"

She lifted a single finger and pointed to the tray that Sadie had moved to the foot of the bed. "Water?"

Tyler stood and carefully slid the tray over Gram's legs until it was within her reach. He picked up the white tumbler, tilting the straw to her lips to help her drink.

A bit of Gemma's heart melted as she witnessed their interaction. For years she'd sworn not to let Tyler get close to her again. Even the smallest memory of him had always led her mind right back to the last time she saw him. She'd worked hard to block that horrible night from her memory. With little success, obviously.

After the way he'd dropped everything to be with her yesterday though, the idea of having him back in her life didn't seem so terrible anymore. She hadn't wanted to contact him, but now she found herself glad she had.

Tyler glanced up from Gram, catching Gemma's eye. One side of his mouth ticked up in a tiny half smile that caused flutters to erupt in her stomach. Blake used to look at her almost exactly that way. Except it had never made her feel all warm and jittery inside like Tyler's gaze did now.

But that half smile had to mean something different coming from him. He didn't have any sort of romantic feelings for her. The mental reminder squeezed her heart a little.

And yet, something about the way he studied her made it impossible for her to look away.

"Here we are," Sadie sang as she reentered the room.

Gemma jumped at the cheerful pronouncement, and she managed to pull her eyes from his as the nurse adjusted the glass vase full of flowers on the windowsill.

Sadie stepped back and surveyed the arrangement with her hands on her hips. "They sure add a little sunshine in here, don't they?" Turning to face the room, she hunched her shoulders a little in apology. "Oh, I'm so sorry. I didn't realize she was asleep."

Gemma glanced at Gram, who was, in fact, asleep. She hadn't even made it an hour since her last nap. Dr. Fields had assured Gemma that fatigue was a common side effect of strokes and that sleep was an important step in the brain's healing process. It was hard not to worry, though. Gram was always so vibrant, even at her age. Seeing her so frail and vulnerable was a painful reminder that her life was winding down.

At least she seemed to be sleeping peacefully.

Careful not to disturb her rest, Gemma took Gram's hand hanging off the side of the bed. She gave it a gentle squeeze and tucked it underneath the thin blanket.

"I'll be back one more time to check on her before I end my shift," Sadie said barely above a whisper. "But if you need anything, feel free to hunt me down."

Gemma nodded her understanding, and the nurse left.

"I should probably go so she can rest," Tyler said. "I only wanted to see how she was doing."

"I'm glad you came," Gemma said. And she meant it. "That was really thoughtful of you."

"What can I say? I'm a thoughtful guy." He winked, and the side of his mouth twisted up in another half smile. But this one wasn't the same as the one he gave Gemma earlier. If she was interpreting it correctly, this one seemed almost flirty.

A quiet giggle snuck out, even as she wondered about the look. She didn't remember Tyler being a flirt when they were younger. Was it possible for someone to change that drastically as they aged? She'd seen him flirt with other girls, but it had always felt about as wonderful as the time she'd split her chin open on a rock after falling off her bike.

Awkwardness settled over the room as they sat in silence. Tyler watched her with his head cocked to the side as if he expected her to speak. The problem was she had no idea what to say. Her brain was going a mile a minute, and still, nothing intelligible was coming to her.

Finally, he stood. "Well, I guess I'll be going. I'll stop by later. If that's okay, of course," he added quickly.

"Sure," Gemma said absent-mindedly, still unable to make sense of the change between them.

He nodded once, gave her one last lingering glance, and turned to go.

Gemma watched him exit the room, then blew out a heavy breath and settled more comfortably in her chair for an afternoon of solitude. But as the seconds ticked by, echoing to the beat of the beeping of Gram's heart rate monitor, the quiet seemed to scream a little too loudly.

Gemma was tired of being alone. Tired of fighting to rein in her spiraling thoughts. She was still uncomfortable around Tyler, but the short time he'd sat with her in the waiting room yesterday had provided the only bit of true relief she'd felt since arriving at the hospital. As much as she hated to admit it, having his company a little longer might be a good thing.

She took another look at Gram, hesitant to leave her side. But it would only be for a few minutes. And with Gram asleep, Gemma's absence would surely go unnoticed.

She rose from her chair and tucked the blanket underneath Gram's chin before hurrying from the room. "Tyler!" she shouted when she spotted him at the end of the hall.

He stopped right before stepping onto the escalator. Turning, he shoved his hands into the pockets of his jeans, watching her as she caught up to him.

"What's up?" he asked when she was close enough to converse comfortably.

Tears stung Gemma's eyes before she could stop them. The curiosity in Tyler's handsome features immediately flashed to concern, and he reached out for her. As she stepped into him, he slid one of his hands behind her head, bringing it to rest against his shirt. She melted into his embrace, soaking in his citrusy cologne and the solid muscle of his shoulder against her cheek, letting it soothe her. Unlike the hugs they'd shared lately, this one felt different.

Comfortable.

Safe.

Like their hugs before that stupid kiss. And yet, not. Gah, no wonder she was so confused.

"It's okay," he whispered, stooping so his mouth was close to her ear. "Your grandma is going to be okay."

Gemma closed her eyes, letting his words take root in her mind and heart. She knew he couldn't predict the future. Even though Dr. Fields said Gram's prognosis was good, she wasn't out of the woods yet. Still, Tyler's words comforted her. Or maybe it was simply having someone to share her burden.

"Thank you for being so kind to my grandma," she said after

she'd composed herself. "Especially after I've been so awful to you. I'm sorry for the things I said."

"You haven't been too bad." Tyler placed two fingers under her chin and nudged her face upward. "And anyway, it's water under the bridge now."

Gemma swiped at her eyes with her forearm as more moisture leaked out. "Sorry," she said through an embarrassed laugh. "I'm a hot mess right now."

He trailed his hand down her arm, and tingles followed in its path. Finding her hand, he wove his fingers through hers. "You've been through a lot. It's only natural to be a little emotional. Have you talked to your parents yet?"

Gemma nodded against his chest. "They're making arrangements to come down. I'm not sure when they'll get here, but my dad said he'd keep me updated. Gram scolded him for making such a fuss about her though." She rolled her eyes. Dryly, she said, "Even stuck in a hospital bed, she still thinks she can take on the world."

Tyler chuckled. "She's a strong woman, that's for sure. Her granddaughter is the same." He ran his free hand softly up and down her upper arm. "Is there anything I can do for you? What do *you* need?"

His question only served to soften her heart even more. It also made her realize just how much she'd missed him. It both hurt and buoyed her.

"Gram spends most of the time sleeping. I brought a book, but my thoughts are too loud for me to focus on it for more than a few sentences. Usually, I just stare at the wall." She bit her lip. Did she really want to speak the request on the tip of her tongue?

The answer was yes. Yes, she did.

"Will you stay with me for a while?" She hurried to add, "I can help you study since we didn't get around to it the other night."

His face softened. "Of course. I'll stay as long as you'd like me to." He lifted both her hands to his mouth and kissed her knuckles.

Gemma's breath caught. Out of all the times they'd held hands as children, he'd never once done that. She lifted her eyes to his, and warmth trickled through her at the fondness in his expression. What did this mean?

She didn't have much time to contemplate it before he slid an arm around her shoulders and tucked her in close. Shivers sped down her spine as they walked back to Gram's room. But it was his unwavering loyalty that made her heart truly skip a beat. Under his protective hold, the weight of the past seemed to lighten, and a realization dawned on her.

Tyler may not love her the way she always had him, but there was no doubt in her mind that he did care for her. His friendship had been her absolute favorite thing as a child. And she'd missed it the last several years. Missed him. What they had. Letting him in again might not be such a bad thing. After all, she'd had lots of practice hiding her unrequited feelings from him. She shouldn't have too much trouble doing it again.

Chapter Sixteen

Darkness had fallen by the time Tyler arrived home the following Monday. He yawned as he turned into the driveway, not looking forward to the few hours of studying he still had to do. It would be a miracle if he got any sleep at all tonight.

He slung his backpack over his shoulder and headed toward the open garage door, squinting at the harsh white light flooding onto the cement. Inside, Brad was shooting darts at a dartboard hanging on the inner wall of the garage.

"Hey, stranger," he said, lowering the dart in his hand. "Where've you been?"

Tyler set his backpack onto the cement floor, saving his shoulder from the weight of the textbooks inside. "Hospital."

"Again? That's, what, the fourth day in a row?" Brad chucked the dart at the board. It landed in the center of the outer circle with a thunk. "You must really like this girl."

Tyler looped his thumbs through his front belt loops. "We're friends. And she's been worried about Grandma June. She asked me to come visit."

Technically, she only asked him to stay on Saturday. But he chose to take that as an open invitation to visit again. He'd spent most of that day and Sunday with her, playing cards or talking in whispered conversations while Grandma June slept. Or keeping the woman's spirits up when she was awake. Despite Gemma's offer to help him study, very little talk of calculus occurred within the walls of that drab hospital room. Tyler was okay with that, even if it meant struggling through his notes on his own.

When he'd woken up that morning, he'd considered skipping class and work. But even though the doctors were optimistic that

Grandma June would be able to go home within the week, his grades weren't good enough to start missing school. As soon as his shift had ended, however, he'd headed over, only intending to see if Gemma needed anything.

The happiness in her eyes when he walked through the door had tugged at something deep in his core. She'd wanted him there, and spending a few minutes with her hadn't been enough, especially now that she was finally opening up to him again. He would've stayed longer if not for the hours of studying still hanging over his head.

"So, listen," Brad said in a casual tone, pulling Tyler's thoughts away from Gemma. "I was thinking about maybe asking Gemma out. You know, after things settle down with her grandma, of course."

Tyler's eyes flew to his cousin, who was innocently studying the dart he slowly spun with his fingers. "Why would you do that?" He couldn't disguise the slight panic in his question.

Brad lifted a shoulder. "She's cute. And she seemed like fun when she came over. I think we could have a good time."

"She's not your type," Tyler growled through clenched teeth. Brad, go out with Gemma? It would be a frosty day in purgatory before Tyler would let that happen. Wasn't there some clause about that in the guy code? His cousin lived and breathed by the guy code.

Brad sent the dart sailing toward the board. "I'm not picky."

Tyler had the sudden urge to grab one of those darts and chuck it hard at Brad's head. He shoved his hands into his pockets to prevent himself from doing anything that would warrant jail time. "Don't you dare."

Brad arched a blond eyebrow. "Why not? You insist you two are only friends. What's the big deal?"

"The big deal is that she's *my* friend."

"*Friend* being the operative word. Meaning she's free to date. I don't see what the issue is here."

"The issue is that *I* want to date her." His mouth dropped open.

Where did that come from? With wide eyes, he swiveled to face his cousin.

Brad's mouth curved into a satisfied smirk. "And there it is." He approached Tyler's side and thumped him on the shoulder blade. "Glad you could finally catch up, buddy."

Tyler fisted a clump of his own hair as he puffed out a breath. "When did that happen?"

"Are you kidding?" his cousin said incredulously. "I saw it from the very first moment you walked into the kitchen with her ten days ago. The real question is what're you going to do about it?"

Heaving another sigh, Tyler leaned his hip against the shelving unit nailed to the side wall of the garage. "I don't know."

Now that the words were out, he realized they weren't all that surprising. Why hadn't he figured it out before? He was attracted to her, sure. That much was obvious with how often she dominated his mind, the weird way his body reacted the few times he was fortunate enough to touch her ...

But dating her? When had that possibility entered the equation? And how would she even feel about it?

"What am I supposed to do in this situation?" He slid both hands down the sides of his face as he thought. "It's not like I can go up to her and say, 'Hey buddy, old pal'"—he swung his fist in front of his chest, pantomiming slugging a friend on the shoulder—"'what do you say about blowing this friendship into smithereens? Let's make out.'"

Brad snorted out a laugh. "Please, whatever you do, don't say that." He stepped to the dartboard and pulled out the three darts stuck into the cork. Walking over to Tyler, he held one out to him.

Tyler accepted it, running his thumb along the dense metal as he lined up his shot. "She's finally letting me back in again. I don't want to scare her off." Things seemed so much simpler when they were kids. Back when they weren't thinking about romance. They were simply two best buds who did everything together. How was he supposed to navigate this friendship when his heart was now involved? He chucked the dart at the board half-heartedly.

"What was that?" Brad asked in amusement.

Tyler shrugged. "I think I'll stick to baseball." He could land a fastball right in the middle of the strike zone with no problem, but finding a tiny circle in the center of a board used an entirely different set of skills that he didn't have.

Brad tossed the remaining darts onto the small container sitting on the shelving unit and faced his cousin, crossing his arms over his chest. "What about a grand gesture? Chicks eat that stuff up."

It was a good thing Kendall wasn't nearby. She hated when Brad used animal names to refer to women, and she wasn't afraid to call him out whenever he did. But Tyler had to admit that he wasn't too keen on Brad referring to Gemma that way either. "She's not a chick."

Brad raised both his hands in a show of apology.

"A grand gesture, huh?" Tyler wasn't sure about this one. He didn't consider himself a flashy kind of guy. Big declarations of love were never his thing.

Wait … Love? His whole body went cold. He'd barely admitted that he wanted to date her. It had to be too soon to consider it love. Right?

Maybe a grand gesture wasn't the best idea. But he could start with something small, perhaps. Something to put his feelers out there to see whether she'd be open to the idea of a date.

"I'll have to think about that," he said, walking toward the mouth of the garage where the fluorescent lighting illuminated Brad's green Pathfinder in the driveway. He picked up his backpack. "Thanks, man."

"Any time." Brad smacked the button next to the door leading into the laundry room. A loud, grinding sound filled the garage as the mechanical door lowered.

Tyler followed his cousin into the house. "You weren't really planning to ask her out, were you?"

Brad shook his head, his eyes twinkling with mischief. "Nah, you were right. She's not my type. But she's perfect for you."

Tyler clapped him on the shoulder before leaving the kitchen and heading up the stairs. Once in his room, he dropped his bag on the carpet and paced the floor.

Am I seriously considering asking Gemma out?

He'd finally gotten her back after seven years of wondering why she wouldn't return his calls. Was he ready to risk another twist in their friendship? What if she didn't feel the same? Something had stopped her from saying goodbye all those years ago, something that still bothered her now.

His chest tightened as the kiss he'd shared with Cassie came to mind. Given the new direction of his feelings toward Gemma, it was difficult to brush it off as simply a meaningless impulse of a sixteen-year-old boy. But it couldn't be what had caused her to pull away.

Could it?

He'd already lost her once.

He'd do everything in his power never to lose her again.

Chapter Seventeen

Gram's coming home.

Gemma drove back to the house, more weight lifting off her shoulders with each repetition of that thought. The last week had seemed like a weird time warp, and she felt like she was finally reemerging into the real world after a long sleep. She might as well change her name to Rip Van Winkle.

She pulled into the driveway of the house and immediately spotted Tyler, dressed in a gray T-shirt and black basketball shorts, standing to the side of the front door. His body was stretched out to its full length as he hung a beautiful rustic swing to the awning covering the porch. A long, white cushion and an assortment of pillows in varying shades of blue lay off to the side, waiting to be arranged on top of it.

Gemma folded her arms on top of the car's window frame and watched him for a moment, admiring the way the muscles in his arms flexed as he worked.

Her opinion of him had drastically changed over the course of the week. After all he'd done to help, he'd proved that he really was the same kind, considerate Tyler he'd been before. Stopping by every day after school to check on Gram. Showing her care as if she were his own grandma and not a woman he'd only met a couple weeks ago. He'd even picked up Gemma's parents when they'd arrived on Tuesday. But her favorite moments of the last week were just hanging out with him and finally having the chance to talk the way they used to without the awkward barriers.

Gemma slid from the car and approached the porch as Tyler finished attaching the string. His mouth lifted in his signature heart-stopping grin when he spotted her.

"Hey," he said. "I wasn't expecting you. I thought you'd want to be at the hospital when Grandma June got released." She'd called him as soon as they'd received the news that Gram was cleared to come home.

"I needed to grab some clothes for her to change into." Gemma wrapped her arms around her middle, trying to stop the giddy flutters in her stomach. "What's all this?"

He followed her gaze to the swing and gave the chain a gentle tug. "I was thinking that when Grandma June comes home, she might want to sit out here and watch the sun go down. But there isn't anywhere to sit. So, I bought you a swing."

He bought them a swing? But he only worked part-time. There was no possible way his hourly wage created a ton of excess funds, and outdoor furniture didn't come cheap. Yet, he did it anyway. Just to make Gram's life a little easier.

Gemma almost pounced on him. Almost tackled him in the world's tightest hug that could've easily ended with her lips on his. *Keep those feelings firmly buried,* she reminded herself.

Clasping her hands behind her back, she swayed side to side a little, trying to remain casual. After the number of times she'd broken down in tears in front of him, she didn't need to add another question mark to her emotional stability. "You didn't need to do that."

"I know." Those irresistible lips quirked up, unfairly awakening Gemma's desire to explore them. "I wanted to. And I have something for you too."

Curiosity pricked at Gemma, lessening the unwelcome desire to a more manageable level. "What is it?"

Tyler's eyes sparked with mischief. "Hold out your hand and close your eyes."

She complied. A second later, the rustling of heavy fabric came from somewhere off to her side. A zipper opening. Then more rustling. It was amazing what her ears could pick up when her eyes took a back seat.

Turning toward the sound, she slowly opened her eyes a crack as the zipper closed again.

"I know what you're doing," Tyler said, his voice wobbling with a laugh.

"What?" she asked innocently, snapping her lids shut again.

"You're doing that thing where you scrunch your brows so you can get a peek without it looking like your eyes are open."

"You knew about that?"

He made a scoffing sound and she giggled. "Of course I knew. It was so obvious. Cover your face so I know you're not sneaking a peek."

Gemma brought her hand up to her eyes, unable to keep a wide smile from spreading across her mouth. A second later, Tyler placed something in her outstretched hand. The rectangular object was too wide and thick to wrap her fingers all the way around it and felt smooth against her skin.

"Now you can open them."

She glanced down at the bold, red lettering of the Sahne-Nuss bar wrapped in yellow. She arched an eyebrow at Tyler standing in front of her, watching her reaction. "Did you fly to Chile for the day to get this? I know for a fact they don't have these in the grocery store I go to."

He chuckled. "I wish. I meant it when I told you I'd go anywhere in the world for you, but unfortunately, I don't have the time or the money to take random flights to foreign countries."

So, she was right about his money situation. That should've made her feel guilty about the expense of the swing, but his thoughtfulness only touched her more. "Where'd you get it, then?"

"There's an international store just off Main Street that carries them. My sisters and I discovered it when I helped them pick up their couch at the secondhand shop next door."

"You have to show me where this place is." Gemma turned the candy bar in her hand. "Split it with me?"

"Sure." They walked to the swing, and he set the cushion on top of the wood.

"This isn't going to collapse once we sit down, is it?" She tugged on the chain a little, testing its strength.

Tyler shot her a side-eye that was more amused than offended. "Hey, I might be bad at math, but I think I'm pretty good at following instructions."

To prove it, he sat down. Gemma winced a little, expecting him to end up sprawled on his back on the cement. But the swing remained intact. He reached up and yanked on the hem of her shirt, bringing her down next to him.

"Speaking of math," she said, unwrapping the bar, "I never asked how your test went." She broke off a piece of chocolate and handed it to him.

Tyler pushed out a forceful laugh. "Do we have to talk about that now?"

"Was it really that bad?"

"I passed. At least ... barely." He popped the chocolate into his mouth and chewed, drawing her eyes to his strong jaw. "I hate math."

Regret pooled in Gemma's stomach. If she hadn't ditched him the night he'd come over to study, maybe he would've done better. "I'm really sorry. I shouldn't have bailed on you."

He shook his head. "It's okay. Why do I even need it anyway? I don't know many journalists who work with derivatives and integrals. And by *not many,* I mean *none.*"

Gemma knocked his arm with her elbow. "Do you remember all those times you begged me to help you with your math homework back in school? You asked the same question then too."

He smiled down at her. "Now that Grandma June is coming home and your parents are here, I might need to start begging again if I want to pass this class. We didn't even touch my textbook at the hospital. Not that I'm complaining about that much."

"I could possibly help you," she said with a shrug. "But you might have to pay for it."

Tyler clicked his tongue. "Taking advantage of a man in need? You're brutal, Gemma Schalk."

"I have to make a living somehow." She placed a piece of the bar on her tongue, savoring the combination of sweet and salty from the chocolate and almonds. "Remember when we used to stop at the panadería for these on our walk home from school? And you would always bet that I couldn't eat the whole thing by myself?"

"I never understood it," he said, shaking his head. "You could eat half of one and, less than thirty minutes later, be running around the bases. If I ate even a few squares before playing baseball, I'd throw up."

"I'm pretty sure you actually did."

"Shhhh," he hissed, circling an arm around her shoulders to cover her mouth. "I had food poisoning. And you promised never to bring that up again."

Gemma batted his hand away, ignoring the goose bumps rippling down her arms from his touch. "Haven't you ever crossed your fingers behind your back when you made a promise?"

"Brutal *and* deceitful. You weren't lying, Gem. You *have* changed." He winked at her.

She shoved him away, unable to hold back a laugh at his very unmanly giggle. "Hey, you're no saint either." Especially the way he weaseled his way back into her good graces. And the devilish smile he was giving her that made her want to explore the idea of kissing him.

It is not okay to kiss your best friend, she thought, willing the burning in her face to go away. She repeated the phrase in her mind over and over like a Gregorian chant. *It is not okay to kiss your best friend.*

Only after several repetitions did she realize Tyler was staring at her like he was expecting something from her.

"What? Did you say something? My mind must have wandered."

She busied her hands by breaking off another piece of chocolate and popping it in her mouth.

"Oh yeah?" he asked, his voice turning flirty, suggestive. "What were you thinking about?" He angled his body toward her, moving a little closer as a broad grin slid onto his face.

She choked a little, and a piece of almond scratched her throat going down. Had he read her mind? He couldn't possibly know where her thoughts had led.

"Nothing," she said quickly once she'd swallowed. "What were you saying?"

He studied her with a mischievous smirk before taking pity on her. "I just asked how your baseball skills were these days. Do you still play?"

She coughed, dragging her thoughts away from his lips. Yet she was grateful for the change of topic. "Uh, they're pretty nonexistent, actually. I haven't played in years." Not since the day before he'd left Santiago, in fact. But there was no way she was getting into that.

"Really?" His brows furrowed, and he studied her for a drawn-out moment. "That's a shame. You were the best out of all of us."

That forced a snort from Gemma. "Hardly."

"I'm serious," he said, bumping her shoulder. "You were the only one who could get a hit on Parker's slider. And my curveball would still need work if it weren't for you."

Now was the time to steer the conversation away from her. If it continued the way it was going, she might admit too much. And she didn't want to run the risk of confessing that she knew about the kiss. "What about you? How come you're not playing for USC like you always talked about?"

Tyler took the piece of chocolate Gemma handed to him. "Living in Chile kind of set me back since I missed all those years playing in travel leagues and stuff. I pitched for my high school and thought about trying to walk onto the team here, but it's already hard enough to focus on my classes without baseball on top of it. So, it's the summer intramural league for me."

"I'm sorry it didn't work out for you."

"That's alright," he mumbled through the chocolate in his mouth. Then he swallowed hard. "I wouldn't trade those years for anything."

He seriously needed to stop with the half smiles. They had the same effect as dropping her into the center of a volcano. She looked away before her whole heart escaped through her face.

Silence fell over them as they watched the neighbor across the street get into her car and pull out of the driveway.

"I should get back to the hospital," Gemma said after a minute. "They're probably waiting for me."

But she didn't move. The fresh air and sunlight caressing her skin were too relaxing to think about getting up. Not to mention the connection between them right now made her want to bask in this peaceful spot forever. Was she horrible for not feeling a greater urgency to get back to the hospital? Mom and Dad were with Gram. They could wait a few extra minutes so Gemma could enjoy this a little longer.

The rough canvas of Tyler's gray boat shoes rubbed against her bare calf, sending prickles up to her knee. That reaction confused her. He was probably shuffling his feet as he rocked the swing and grazed her leg by accident. Her body's response was completely ridiculous.

Then why didn't he move it back? Did he not realize it was still resting against her skin?

Gemma sat perfectly still, unsure of what to make of all this. The intense looks. The flirty smiles. The little touches. Could it be possible that his feelings for her had changed? That he no longer looked at her as one of his sisters?

She was unable to process even the possibility of it being true. And the giddy zing traveling up her spine wasn't helping. Hoping to ease some of the tension, she hooked her leg around his and tugged it toward her, forcing him to lose his center of gravity on the bench. He drifted to the side.

"What're you doing?" he asked, grabbing the arm of the swing to catch himself.

"Nothing," she said, stifling a snort. She extended her leg toward his again for a second try.

"You're trying to knock me off the swing, aren't you?" He shoved her shoulder a little, though laughter sparkled in his blue eyes. "What are you, five?"

She tried to keep a straight face as she looked down her nose at him, but she was unsuccessful. "Of course not. If I were five, my feet wouldn't touch the ground." She attacked again.

A crack of laughter erupted from him, followed by retaliation. In one fell swoop, he hooked his leg over hers and pulled hard toward him. She lunged away, but the movement only knocked her off-balance. She squeaked as her butt slid off the cushion, sending her down.

Strong arms came around her seconds before her back hit the cement. Her chest heaved with the effort it took to breathe from the exertion. Or maybe it was the fact that Tyler's face hovered inches from hers. Well within kissing range.

"Nice catch." Her voice emerged breathless, and she couldn't pull her eyes away from his.

"Quick reflexes," he said in a husky whisper.

Without breaking eye contact, Tyler lifted her back onto the swing, keeping his hands at her waist, the feel of his touch burning straight through her shirt as if they were touching skin.

His gaze flicked to her mouth, and Gemma's heart thudded hard against her rib cage. *He's going to kiss me.* There was no question about that.

As his face inched closer to hers, the distance disappeared much too quickly, and yet not fast enough. She'd thought about this moment more times than she could count. Dreamed about what his kisses would taste like, the softness of his lips, the feel of being held exactly this way. Never in her wildest imaginings, though, did she ever think it would happen.

But it was! And even through the confusion swirling around her brain, she wanted this. Forcing all her conflicting feelings aside, she closed her eyes. The seconds ticked past as she waited for the fireworks to explode with the connection of their lips.

It was coming. Any second now ...

Tires squealed on the street in front of the house, breaking the spell.

Tyler pulled his hands away. "Who's that?"

Gemma's eyelids flew open when she felt him move back. Face burning, she turned toward the car now parked in front of the house.

The sight of the new arrival getting out of the sedan jolted her from the fog of their almost kiss. "Oh my gosh, it's Cassie." She bolted from the swing, adjusting her shorts that had bunched up while she was sitting. Her flip-flops slapped against the pavement on her way to greet her sister.

"Hey, sis." Cassie, in her straight-legged jeans and designer top, looked as stylish as ever, and not at all like she'd just taken a cross-country flight from New York. She enfolded Gemma in a tight hug. "I'm so glad you're home. I didn't know the address of the hospital, so I thought I'd come here instead. I know, I know. I should've called first, but I wanted to surprise you. Hey, Tyler."

He waved. "It's good to see you."

When he wrapped an arm around Cassie in a side hug, a prick of jealousy sparked in Gemma's stomach. It was an irrational response, she knew. Hadn't she just decided to let go of the past? That meant she couldn't get defensive over a casual greeting. Tyler and Cassie were friends too, after all. They might not have the close relationship Gemma once had with him, but they were still friends. And it was normal for friends to hug.

"Thanks for calling me the other day," Cassie said, flashing her friendly smile at him. "It was so nice to catch up."

The prick clawed its way out of Gemma's stomach and into her chest. He called her? What happened to sending a quick text?

You're being unfair. Cassie wasn't the same boy-chasing girl she used to be. She'd grown up, especially during college. And besides, she was fully committed to her boyfriend. Who'd soon be her fiancé. *Wait a minute …*

"What about Mexico?" Gemma couldn't help asking. "You're supposed to be leaving tomorrow." Had her sister given up her trip with Drew to come?

Cassie shrugged like it was no big deal that she was here instead of packing for her exotic proposal trip, but she couldn't mask the sadness. "I thought it was more important to be with the family right now," she said simply.

"How does Drew feel about it?"

"He's not happy." Cassie lowered her gaze to the sidewalk, and her shoulders shuddered a little. When she looked up again, her smile was firmly back in place. "But he'll get over it. It'll be fine."

There was something below the surface of her forced cheerfulness that she wasn't admitting. And Gemma didn't like the way her own stomach bubbled right then, though she couldn't say whether it had to do with sadness over Cassie's demeanor when she'd mentioned Drew's unhappiness or the fact that she was standing next to Tyler. Seeing them together now must be messing with Gemma's brain, because the image of their moonlight kiss jumped into her memories, squeezing her heart painfully.

And along with it came all the harmful thoughts attacking her self-worth that had plagued her in the days following Tyler's departure.

Chapter Eighteen

Seven Years Earlier

July

"Are you sure you're okay?" Cassie asked for the millionth time on the short walk around the corner to the panadería.

"I'm fine," Gemma said through clenched teeth. She was beginning to regret inviting her sister to come along on this outing. If not for their parent's buddy-system rule any time they left the house, she'd have gone alone. It didn't matter that she was sixteen and had lived in Lo Barnachea for over half her life. Safety first, Mom always said. Even if it meant hanging out with a traitor.

How could her sister betray her like that? Tyler was *Gemma's* best friend. Despite how boy crazy Cassie was, he should be off-limits.

On the other hand, Cassie was still her sister. And Gemma still had to live with her. It didn't matter how angry she was over what happened, they'd be connected for life. She couldn't say the same for Tyler.

"It's just that I heard you sniffling in your sleep last night." Cassie wouldn't let the subject drop as they arrived at the bakery. "Are you getting sick?"

Gemma shook her head and yanked the door open, the warm scent of baking bread greeting her when she walked inside. The bakery wasn't large and consisted of two glass-covered displays running the entire length of two walls. Near the entrance, a case of chocolate bars and other candies sat ready to entice anyone who came in. She passed right by the display without giving it even the slightest glance. She'd never look at another Sahne-Nuss bar without thinking of Tyler.

"Buenos días," the proprietor called cheerfully from behind one of the displays holding an assortment of Chilean pastries.

"Buenos días," she repeated, though the greeting sounded hollow even to her.

Cassie, on the other hand, gave an enthusiastic wave. "Hola, Señor Morales. Cómo estás?"

Señor Morales responded with his usual welcome smile. "Muy bien, gracias." His gaze fell on Gemma, and his smile dimmed. "Qué pasa?" he asked, his tone full of grandfatherly concern, most likely a product of having watched the girls grow up.

Jorge Morales and his wife, Camila, had been running the panadería since long before the Schalks had moved to Santiago. Possibly before Gemma was even born. For reasons she didn't know, the Moraleses were never able to have children, but they endeared themselves to every kid who entered their shop. She and Tyler often lingered after school to exchange language lessons with the kind man. While he taught them Spanish words they didn't already know, they helped him practice his English.

Stop thinking about Tyler, she scolded her brain. "I'm fine," she mumbled, forcing her mouth up a smidge. She was a long way from fine.

"Ah, come, come," he said in a soothing voice, motioning for them to step up to the counter for a closer look. "I know what you need." Sliding the glass door open, he pulled out two flat, circular rolls and handed them to both girls. "Pan amasado. I bake this morning. Eat while they're hot."

"Gracias," the girls said in unison. Gemma broke off a piece of the Chilean bread and slid it into her mouth. The warm, fluffy goodness practically melted on her tongue.

They decided to share an order of sopaipillas. The deep-fried dough that resembled a beignet was one of Gemma's favorite snacks. After handing Señor Morales some money, they watched him place several in a paper bag along with a small container of honey for dipping.

Armed against the foggy chill with sugar and carbs, they stepped back outside. Neither of those things would keep them warm on their walk home, but there was something to be said about carbs soothing a broken heart.

"I still don't know why you had the sudden urge to come here now," Cassie said as a gust of wind knocked her back a step. "I thought you would've wanted to say goodbye to Tyler. I know they were planning to leave early."

No, Gemma did *not* want to say goodbye to him. Tyler Abernathy was dead to her.

"We said goodbye last night." She kept walking, keeping her focus away from her sister. Reaching into the bag she held, she pulled out a sopaipilla and took a bite, hoping to disguise the wobbling of her chin.

Unfortunately, luck wasn't on her side.

"Oh, Gem!" Cassie's arms wrapped around her from the side, the hug trapping Gemma in a near chokehold.

Startled by the sudden movement, her comfort carbs flew from her hand, tumbling to the ground. "I was planning to eat that," she muttered, staring longingly at the ruined pastry on the pavement. A stray dog wandered over to inspect the potential treat.

Cassie didn't let go, not even after they'd resumed walking. "I understand completely why you're sad. When Cara left, I was a mess for weeks. You remember, don't you?"

Cara was Cassie's best friend. Her dad had worked at the US embassy until last December when their family moved back to Washington D.C.

Gemma leaned her head against Cassie's shoulder, letting her sister think she was simply sad about her best friend moving away. That was better than the embarrassment of being brutally rejected by the boy she'd been in love with for six years.

They walked this way until they reached the corner that led onto their street. A palpable emptiness resonated from the Abernathy's property as they passed by it. Normally, the bustle of laughter and happy squeals from Tyler's siblings rang above the stucco wall surrounding the property. The only thing ringing now was silence.

Good riddance, Gemma thought as they reached their own gate. She punched in the code to unlock it and pushed the door open. However, an unwelcome pang of sadness took root in her heart as she gave one last look at the empty property next door. She forced it away. Tyler was officially out of her life, and she was better for it. If she kept repeating that to herself, maybe eventually she'd believe it.

"There you are," Mom said when they entered the kitchen. She still wore her pink, fuzzy bathrobe, her usual Saturday morning attire since she didn't have to teach classes. Turning off the tap, she set the rinsed plate in the drying rack before facing the girls. "Tyler stopped by a little bit ago. He was hoping to say goodbye. He said he'd call you when he gets to Miami."

Gemma set the bag of sopaipillas on the table and nodded to acknowledge Mom's comment, then continued to the stairs without responding. As she climbed up to her room, she overheard Cassie mention her name, though she didn't stop to hear what was said. It was hard enough keeping the tears at bay whenever Tyler's name was mentioned, and that seemed to be all everyone wanted to talk about.

When she entered her room, she kicked at a pair of Cassie's designer jeans lying on the floor by the doorway before flopping onto her bed. Her eyes stung with new moisture, and she furiously blinked it away. One pesky tear escaped and trickled down her cheek. *Dang it, Tyler!* Even out of the way, he was still affecting her. How could one boy make her feel so unlovable?

She knew that she wasn't the kind of girl guys thought of romantically. Boys didn't fall in love with girls who could beat them in a home run contest or strike them out in three pitches. They didn't fall for girls who wore basketball shorts and bushy braids.

Nope, guys liked girls like Cassie. Beautiful, flirty, and feminine. The very opposite of Gemma.

She sat up, catching her reflection in the mirror on Cassie's vanity. She brought a hand up to finger the frizzy curls spilling out of her ponytail. If Tyler couldn't love her for who she was, would there be anyone who could?

Maybe it was time for a change.

As she got up from her bed, her eyes fell on the baseball lying on the carpet nearby. She hadn't bothered putting it back on her dresser after Tyler had dropped it last night. She picked it up, memories flashing through her mind as she rotated it in her hands. Baseball games in the grassy field a few streets over, playing catch with him in their backyards, teaching him how to throw a knuckleball.

What used to fill her with happiness were all just painful reminders of her inadequacies now.

I'll never play another baseball game again.

More tears slid down her cheek as she walked over to her closet and pulled out her backpack. Turning it over, she gave it a few good shakes. Pencils, pens, and spiral notebooks dropped onto the floor.

She brought it to her bed and placed it right side up on her blankets, then tossed the baseball inside. Next, she took her glove from its spot on her desk and shoved it in as well.

She stood back and looked around, her hands on her hips. Spotting her dresser, she marched over to it and yanked open the third drawer down. She pulled out her favorite pair of basketball shorts, green and yellow with the University of Oregon—her parents' alma mater—logo stitched at the hem. After staring at it for only a moment, she stuffed them in the backpack too.

Out came more clothing items: shorts, sweats, Tyler's Miami Marlins sweatshirt she never got around to giving back. Anything that couldn't be considered girly had to go. From this moment on, Gemma Schalk was turning over a new leaf. No longer would she be considered just one of the guys.

Cassie entered the room as Gemma finished her purge and was struggling to zip up the overstuffed backpack. "What are you doing?" she asked, cocking her head curiously to the side, one eyebrow arched.

"Nothing." Gemma carried the bag to the closet and tossed it inside. She'd take it out to the trash later. Before facing her sister again, she blew out a silent breath. Now that Cassie was here, it was time to initiate the next part of her plan. "Cassie?"

"What's up?" Her sister walked over to her dresser and picked up a tube of shimmery lip gloss.

Gemma put most of her weight on one foot, then shifted to the other foot. "I was wondering." She cleared her throat. "Do you ... think ..." She trailed off and cleared her throat again. Why did it feel like something was stuck in there?

Cassie paused in swiping some gloss over her lips and turned away from the mirror to fix her sister with a curious look. "What is it?"

Just say it. After a brief pause, Gemma pushed the words out so fast they sounded like one. "Wouldyoumindteachingme-howtodomyhair?"

Her twin gave a surprised laugh. "What?"

Gemma took another breath and forced herself to slow down. "What I mean to say is, I don't understand how you can make your hair look like you didn't just stick your finger in a light socket. Will you teach me how?"

A gleeful shriek escaped Cassie, and she tossed the tube of lip gloss onto the vanity. It rolled onto the floor and underneath the dresser.

"Oh, I've been waiting for this day!" Prancing over to Gemma, she threw her arms around her. "Can I do your makeup too? I have this eyeshadow that is perfect for your skin tone." She hurried back to her vanity and started searching through her impressive makeup case.

"Can't we just stick to a little mascara?" Gemma asked timidly.

Cassie didn't stop pulling out lip gloss, brushes, and some kind of skin-colored glass bottle. "Nonsense. Come sit. I'm going to make you gorgeous."

Gemma shuffled over to the vanity with stiff legs, regretting the last two minutes. What had she gotten herself into? There was no stopping Cassie when she got excited about something. Gemma had a feeling she was in for more primping than she'd ever had in her entire life.

Heaven help her.

Chapter Nineteen

"And then her sister showed up right as we were about to kiss," Tyler told Brad, filling him in on what had happened with Gemma yesterday afternoon. He turned back to the stove and flipped over the omelet cooking in the skillet.

Brad whistled through his teeth, the sound long and low. "That's some story. Dude, you might be slow on the uptake, but when you finally figure out how you feel about a girl, you really move fast."

"I didn't plan to kiss her. It just happened. Well, almost." Tyler bit down on his bottom lip to hide his smile. If only Cassie hadn't ruined the moment.

He'd tried to hold back. Really, he had. But as he'd held Gemma in his arms, drinking in the warm longing in her hazel eyes, all self-control took a back seat to the burning desire of his heart. And when her beautiful eyes fluttered closed like she wanted it too? He was a goner.

"So, when's the first date?" Brad asked before funneling a large spoonful of Cheerios into his mouth.

Tyler switched off the stove and scooped the omelet onto the plate he'd retrieved from the cabinet above him. "Don't know." He joined his cousin at the island.

"Are you kidding me?" Brad dropped his spoon into his bowl, splashing milk and soggy cereal onto the table. "All that jealous rage when I mentioned possibly asking her out, and now you're not even going to go through with it? Come on, bruh." He grabbed Tyler's phone lying on the marble in front of them and held it out to him. "You gotta text her. Better yet, call her."

Tyler sawed off a piece of the omelet with his fork before glancing up at Brad's expectant look. "It's more complicated than that. Her grandma just got home from the hospital, her parents are here, and Cassie … And they're all trying to figure out what comes next. She's got a lot on her plate right now."

"That's why you need to take her out," Brad said, leaving the island and heading over to the sink. He dropped his bowl inside before facing Tyler again. "You've got the perfect opportunity here to get her mind off all that stress."

He had a point with that. Still, a nagging worry entered Tyler's mind. "I don't know, man. It's a delicate situation. A date with me isn't like any other date. It'll change the dynamic of our friendship. We'll be crossing the bridge between friends to … more than friends. We'll never be the same again. She doesn't need that pressure while dealing with everything else." And what if she said no?

"Your friendship is on unstable ground to begin with. Besides, you almost kissed her. What do you really have to lose?"

Score another point for Brad. Still, Tyler wondered about the possibility that she'd only been caught up in the spontaneity of the moment. Maybe the whole thing was a fluke. These feelings were so new to him that he was having a hard time deciphering what was real as well. Their friendship had improved over the last week, but it was nowhere near the level of comfort they'd shared before.

But he wanted more. More of her. More time to explore these deepening feelings he had for her. And definitely more opportunities to kiss her. And the only way he'd be able to do that was if he could get her alone. A difficult feat with her family around.

Tyler shoveled the last bite of omelet into his mouth. As he chewed, he made a decision. He had to take the risk.

He waited another hour while he showered and got ready for the day before calling Gemma. With the phone braced against his shoulder, he walked into his room, the ringing echoing in his ear. For a moment, he didn't think she was going to answer. But then the phone clicked, and a beat of silence followed before she spoke.

"Hi," she said by way of greeting.

Her beautiful voice brought an immediate smile to his face. "Hey. How's Grandma June today?"

"Um, hang on." The voices in the background faded suddenly, and Tyler realized she must have gone into a different room. "She's okay. We're finishing up breakfast now. She was able to eat a little bit."

"I'm glad to hear it," Tyler said, though Grandma June wasn't the person he was truly concerned about now. He could hear the heaviness in Gemma's voice. "And how are you doing?"

She didn't answer right away. The only sound came from some feedback on the line. He lowered the phone from his ear to check if the call had dropped, but the timer at the top of the screen still ticked away the seconds. He returned the phone to his ear.

"Gemma?"

"I'm fine."

He frowned. Her tone didn't inspire much confidence in her answer. Was the stress of Grandma June's health weighing on her? For the first time since making his decision to ask her out, Tyler doubted the wisdom of following Brad's advice. She didn't need any more pressure heaped onto her shoulders.

A little voice popped into his head that sounded more like his own than his cousin's. *You'll regret it if you don't take a chance.* That was all he needed to spur himself into action.

"Do you need to get away for a few hours? I'd love to take you on a little adventure to get your mind off everything." *A little adventure?* He sounded like he was nine again, about to take his younger sisters on a "trek" to the end of the street to give Mom a break. Why hadn't he asked Gemma to see a movie, or go to lunch, or … to a baseball game?

That's it!

The Trojans were playing in Arizona this weekend, but he was sure they had a few home games coming up next week. A baseball game was the perfect way to take Gemma's mind off the stress concerning Grandma June's health. Of course, he'd have to think of something else for them to do today.

"Actually ..." Gemma's hesitation broke through Tyler's mental planning. "I can't hang out today. I'm ... just so busy."

His hopes dimmed a bit, but the memory of their almost kiss kept him going. He understood her hesitation. At least, he thought he did. Now that Grandma June was home from the hospital, Gemma's role had shifted from supportive and concerned family member to caregiver. True, she had her parents and Cassie there to help, but eventually they'd all have to return home, and knowing Gemma, she was already thinking about that.

But he didn't need any fancy dates. He simply wanted to be with her. And he couldn't ignore this almost desperate need to make her life even a little easier.

"How can I help?" he asked.

She blew out a breath. "I don't know, Ty. I told my dad I'd pick up Gram's prescription and go to the store since I haven't had the chance to since she's been in the hospital. I'm sorry. It's really not a good time. Maybe later, okay? I have to go."

"Gemma, wait," he pushed out before she could hang up. He didn't like the amount of stress he heard in her voice. "I'll pick up the prescription."

She made a grunt of refusal. "I can't ask you to do that. You've already done so much. And you have a lot on your plate too."

"You're not asking me to do this. I'm offering," Tyler insisted. "And before you say anything else, it's not an imposition or an inconvenience, or anything like that. The only thing I have going on today is some studying, but we both know I'll do anything I can to get out of it. If it's not the prescription, put me to work some other way. I won't stop asking until you do."

She snorted, and he was sure he heard a little sob behind it. The sound tugged at his sympathies, solidifying his need to relieve her burdens. "You were always annoyingly helpful growing up." The smile behind the words was obvious. He could feel it, even if he couldn't see it.

"You know you liked it." Then he softened his tone. "Please, Gem. Let me help."

Tyler held his breath as he waited for her response. Seconds passed in silence while she mulled it over. Why was she being so resistant to his help? She seemed happy to see him whenever he came to visit over the week. What had changed?

It had to be the kiss. Maybe he was moving too fast. He hoped she wasn't rethinking everything.

"Okay," she said finally, the word sounding unsure. "I'll text you the address of her pharmacy. They open at nine thirty on Sundays."

Tyler smiled. It wasn't a glowing acceptance of his offer to help, but it was an acceptance. And he'd get to see her again, however reluctant she sounded. He only hoped that, in time, he'd be able to prove to her that his feelings were real and that going on a date with him wouldn't be such a bad thing.

Chapter Twenty

Not even a healthy dose of vitamin D could free Gemma from the confines of her overworking mind. As she pushed Gram's wheelchair around the block only hours after her phone conversation with Tyler, she couldn't help replaying the previous afternoon. It had been nothing short of amazing.

She still couldn't believe he'd bought her a swing.

Well, he'd bought Gram a swing. The care and concern he continued to offer her grandma touched Gemma deeply.

And he'd almost kissed her! She'd never forget the way he looked at her as his face inched slowly closer. His intense stare had burned a hole right through her crumbling defenses, causing a yearning inside her that would only be filled with his lips on hers. She'd wanted to kiss him—no, *needed* to kiss him—to know if it was as wonderful as she'd always imagined.

She should be lounging in a comfy, golden-framed chair on cloud nine right now, being fanned with palm fronds by people in togas. How many birthday candles had she wished on over the years for him to finally realize she was so much more than a friend? There was no point adding up the number, but it had been a lot. Never had she hoped for something so desperately, in fact.

But ever since Cassie had arrived in Buena Hills, Gemma couldn't help rethinking everything.

You're only opening yourself up to more hurt, Gemma thought, gripping the handles of the wheelchair so tightly that the skin on her knuckles turned white. She'd vowed seven years ago never to let him hurt her again. That sixteen-year-old girl who'd cried herself to sleep hadn't been mature enough to understand that changing herself completely simply because one boy didn't return her feelings wouldn't change a thing if she didn't love herself as she was. She'd done a lot of soul-searching since then, and she'd like to think she wouldn't make the same mistake again.

At least the weather was nice. The slight breeze tickled Gemma's skin, lifting her curls off her shoulders. That, and getting out to stretch her legs—especially after all the time she'd spent at the hospital—lifted her somber mood a little, even if it failed to shut off her brain. She needed this walk as much as Gram did.

When a heavier wind whipped through, Gemma stopped walking and leaned around the side of the chair to look into her grandmother's face. "Are you still doing okay, Gram? If you're too cold, we can turn back. I'm sure lunch will be ready soon."

Gram's mouth turned up slightly as she watched a robin, its orange belly puffed out, hopping along the pavement in front of them. Then she turned her smile to her granddaughter. "I'm doing fine, dear. Let's go a little farther. It's such a lovely day." She patted Gemma's hand where it rested on the wheelchair's side handle.

It was hard to see Gram without her usual snappy spark. They were lucky she hadn't lost her ability to communicate, and Doctor Fields had been confident that physical therapy would help her regain her mobility with time. They had so much to be grateful for. Yet Gemma could tell Gram struggled with her new reality. Knowing she'd found some peace in being outside provided Gemma a tiny bit of relief.

Sandwiching Gram's hand between her own, she said, "Whenever you're ready to turn back, you just say the word, okay?"

At her grandmother's nod, Gemma stood up straight again and continued walking. The robin, having stopped to pick at something in the nearby grass, resumed its hopping, keeping a few feet ahead of them, but not bothered enough to take off flying.

She breathed in the sweet, intoxicating scent from the wisteria growing in the yard they passed. Closing her eyes, she lifted her face to the sky as she strolled slowly down the sidewalk, letting the sun's rays warm her cheeks.

Gram was right. It was much too nice a day to spend inside. Perfect weather for eating lunch on the porch swing.

Gemma stopped, her thoughts immediately returning to yesterday. To the almost kiss that shouldn't have happened.

But it had felt oh so amazing at the time. Ugh. Why couldn't she get rid of all these conflicting feelings? She wasn't usually this wishy-washy. She'd graduated at the top of her class for crying out loud. Made it into a master's program at a good school. Yet when it came to Tyler, she couldn't seem to figure out her own mind.

Wonderful, she thought, rolling her eyes at herself.

She spotted Tyler's used Honda parked at the curb while they were still two doors down. Her stomach churned at the prospect of seeing him again. Just yesterday, she was so happy when she'd arrived home to find him on her doorstep. What a difference twenty-four hours could make.

The discomfort in her stomach only grew as she and Gram turned into the driveway and the front porch came into view. Tyler was sitting in the exact spot he'd occupied the day before, rocking the swing gently with his feet. On the other end, Cassie perched sideways, facing him, her left leg pulled up underneath her thigh. Her easy laugh carried across the breeze, and Gemma ground her teeth.

Seriously, girl. Let. It. Go. Cassie and Tyler weren't even sitting that close to each other. A couple feet separated them—large enough to fit another person in between. Them sharing the swing shouldn't cause such an intense visceral reaction. *Whatever happened to hiding your feelings?*

She continued pushing Gram up the driveway. The motion must have alerted Tyler to their arrival because he turned toward them, his face breaking into an immediate smile. He popped up from the swing and made his way over to them.

"Hey, there you are," he said, helping to lift Gram's wheelchair over the single step onto the porch. "I brought the prescription. Cassie took it inside."

Gemma forced herself to meet his eyes. "Thank you."

He greeted Gram with a peck on her cheek like he'd done every day she was in the hospital. It wasn't lost on Gemma that he still didn't know her very well and yet he treated her as if she were his own grandma. Not many people could do that.

"Hey, Grandma June, it's good to see you so perked up," he said, patting her arm, careful not to jostle the brace supporting her broken wrist. "Did you enjoy your walk?"

Gram was putty in his hands, as she had been all week. "It was lovely."

She gestured with a slightly shaky finger from her good hand for him to come closer. Tyler went down on one knee to converse with her. Gemma inclined her head toward them to hear.

"Thank you for being such a boon to my Gemma this week. I worry about her sometimes, not knowing anyone here."

The side of his mouth lifted in a crooked smile that made Gemma's heart skip a beat, even though it wasn't directed at her.

"It's my absolute pleasure," he said, sincerity in every word. "There's nothing I wouldn't do for our Gemma." His gaze shifted to Gemma, and he winked.

Our Gemma.

Suddenly, she felt as though her whole body was being cooked from the inside out. Her heart pounded, and she wouldn't be surprised if beads of sweat were forming across her forehead.

Thankfully, the front door opened right then, and Mom poked her head out, saving Gemma from having to come up with a response.

"Oh good," Mom said. "You're back just in time. Lunch is ready."

"Wonderful." The word came out pitchy, and Gemma cleared her throat. "I'm starving."

Judging by the tilt of her head, Cassie picked up on Gemma's discomfort immediately. At least she didn't say anything. Twin code insisted she keep it a secret. She turned to Tyler. "Do you want to stay?"

"I'd love to." Unfortunately, he seemed to have noticed Gemma's discomfort as well. He watched her with furrowed brows for a minute before looking away and addressing Mom. "Is that okay?"

She smiled at him. "Of course. I made chicken salad, and there's plenty. We'd love to have you join us."

Moving aside so Tyler could wheel Gram into the house, she then led the way through the living room, disappearing into the kitchen. Cassie followed them, and Gemma, dragging her feet, brought up the rear.

She entered the kitchen just as Dad was lifting his mother carefully from her wheelchair to sit at the table. Tyler had abandoned his post as Gram's dutiful sentry to help Mom dish out plates of chicken salad and asparagus. Once everyone was served, they all sat down to eat.

Lunch was an uncomfortable affair. At least for Gemma. Tyler chatted easily with Cassie and her parents—with occasional comments from Gram. Dad seemed particularly interested in Tyler's post-graduation plans to study international journalism and asked him about the classes he was currently taking for his minor in global studies. He teased Cassie, making her laugh. No one seemed to notice Gemma's inability to free herself from her overanalyzing mind.

What were Tyler's intentions with Cassie? What were *Cassie's* intentions with *Tyler?* How did Drew fit into all of this? And why was Tyler so persistent in wanting to help? Gemma had tried to brush him off earlier, claiming she needed to focus on Gram and spend time with her family, but really, she needed space from him to sort out her own thoughts.

As soon as she'd swallowed her last bite, she popped up from the table and began cleaning up the leftovers. Cassie excused herself when her phone buzzed, claiming she needed to talk to Drew, and Mom soon left to help Gram up the stairs to her room for a rest. When Dad disappeared into the living room to catch up on some work, Gemma was left with only Tyler in the kitchen. A nervous flutter danced around her insides.

Talk about déjà vu.

It wasn't long before he joined her at the counter, where she was spooning the leftover chicken salad into a Tupperware container.

"Need some help cleaning up?" he asked, handing her the lid.

She flinched. Seriously, why was she like this? He hadn't made her this uncomfortable since she'd first discovered he lived in Buena Hills. "No, I got it."

She fitted the lid on top of the chicken salad and pressed down to seal the container. All but one corner closed. When she pushed on that corner, the opposite one popped up. She tried again with the same result. What was wrong with this thing?

With both hands, she jammed the stubborn corners onto the container, trying to get them both to click. No luck. Squeezing them with her hands, she grunted in frustration that they refused to conform to her will.

"Are you okay?" Tyler asked in obvious concern.

Gemma spared him a brief glance. "Mm-hmm. Of course. Why wouldn't I be?" She went back to wrestling with the Tupperware container.

"Well, for one thing, that chicken salad doesn't stand a chance against you in a WWE matchup." He took the container from her, and his hand brushed hers, sending a tingle up her arm. After lifting the lid completely off the salad, he fitted it on top again and pressed down, sealing the sides, including the uncooperative corner. He handed it back to her. "And for another thing, I can tell something is bothering you."

Gemma set the container onto the counter, then collapsed against the granite with a heavy sigh. "I don't know what's wrong with me," she admitted. It wasn't a lie. She *didn't* know why she was reacting this way. Completely irrational and nonsensical. Even if he brought this out of her, it shouldn't be this way.

What Tyler did next shouldn't have surprised her, but it did. He wrapped his arms around her, enfolding her in a hug that was equal parts comforting and enticing. Her breath came quicker and shorter, her pulse thudding like a bass in a nightclub.

Relax, she thought, taking a deep, cleansing breath. Tucking her head underneath his chin, she rested her cheek against him, breathing in his alluring scent. Something earthy with a hint of citrus. As she forced her eyes closed, all the doubts that had consumed her for the past twenty-four hours began to fade. Standing in his arms this way had the same effect it did when he'd held her at the hospital, as if he could protect her from all the scary things happening in her life.

She could almost forget that *he* was the scary thing in her life right now. Well, not *him* per se, but her growing feelings for him and the uncertainty of his feelings for her.

"I really wish you'd let me take you on that adventure," he said, the words vibrating against her ear, which was pressed against his clavicle. "I think it would do you some good to get away for a bit."

She smiled at his word choice. "I might have to change my mind simply because you've used the term *little adventure* twice in the same day." She remembered Mrs. Abernathy used to take her kids— Gemma had always been included—on excursions all the time when they lived in Chile. Tyler had rolled his eyes every time she'd called them that, so it was endearing to hear him use the phrase now.

He chuckled. "Hey, whatever works, I say. I think you're going to like it."

"What do you have in mind?" Gemma felt a little weird to still be hugging him, but she tamped down on the feeling and rested her arms a little tighter around his middle.

For what it was worth, he didn't seem in any hurry to pull away either, which should've added to the confusion in Gemma's mind. But it didn't.

"I have tickets to the USC baseball game on Wednesday," he said. "I'd like to take you."

A baseball game? That wasn't what Gemma was expecting. Her

stomach swooped straight to her toes. When he'd asked her about her baseball skills yesterday, she hadn't wanted to get into the reason for giving up everything to do with the sport, and she wasn't too keen on the reminder that the game she used to love was tainted because of him. So, she decided to address the second issue that was causing her nerves to percolate under her skin.

"That sounds an awful lot like a date." She finally pulled back and dropped her hands from around his middle.

Tyler seemed as nervous as she felt. Lowering his face, he brought a hand up to rub the back of his neck before lifting just his eyes to look at her. "That's because ... it is."

His words forced her to suck in a breath. Best friends weren't supposed to date. True, it was becoming difficult to explain his friendliness as just being happy to have her back in his life—especially after yesterday. But a date?

In case the situation wasn't awkward enough, she laughed. Not a humorous laugh. It was more of a nervous twitter that she immediately wished she could take back. "Us ... go on a date? Is that even a good idea?"

"It's a brilliant idea," Cassie said from the bottom stair, and Gemma jumped, then whirled to face her. How long had she been in the room?

"I don't know ..." Gemma started. "Mom and Dad might need my help."

Cassie eyed her with a mixture of curiosity and defiance. "I gave up Mexico to come here and help. Go. Have fun. We'll be fine here." She shifted her gaze to Tyler, her smile turning into a conspiratorial smirk.

Gemma knew her sister well enough to figure out that she was scheming. She turned to Tyler and caught the end of a silent conversation on his end, then a wink. She glanced at Cassie again, who nodded back at him.

Am I missing something? Gemma thought, shifting uncomfortably on her feet. Tyler and Cassie seemed to be in cahoots, which should have upended her, but deep in her core, she suspected it had everything to do with her.

Before she could voice her confusion out loud, she felt Tyler's hand connect with hers, drawing her attention to him. "I know you said you weren't really into baseball anymore. I don't understand why, but I promise it will be fun. Please say you'll come. We don't have to stay the whole time if you don't want to."

Gemma hesitated for a second longer, studying each one of her fingers encased in his. Out of excuses, she finally lifted her eyes to meet his. His hopeful gaze brought a reluctant smile to her face. "Okay, you got me. I'll go to the game with you."

"Awesome," he said, flashing a triumphant grin in her direction, making her laugh. "We'll have a blast. You'll see."

Gemma hoped he was right.

Chapter Twenty-One

Gemma shook out her hands as she walked into the living room on Wednesday, already dressed for her date with Tyler. Her sneaker squeaked on the hardwood floor, alerting Cassie and Gram, who were sitting next to each other on the couch.

Cassie stopped scrolling through her phone to scrutinize her sister's appearance. "Is that really what you're wearing?" she asked, scrunching up her nose.

"What's wrong with what I'm wearing?" Gemma glanced down at the baseball tee and denim shorts that made up her outfit.

A strangled sound came from Cassie's throat as she rose from the couch. It sounded a little like she'd just gagged on salt water. "You look like you're on your way to the park to hit some fly balls, not going on a date with a hot guy."

Gemma cast her eyes to the ceiling. "I know you're the fashion guru in this family, but this is the kind of outfit a person usually wears to a baseball game." Granted, she hadn't been to one in years. "It's not like he's taking me for a fancy dinner and dancing."

"It doesn't matter. Even if you're *going* to a baseball game, you're not *playing* in one. You can still look cute."

Before Gemma could provide a counterargument, her sister grabbed her hand and began dragging her to the stairs. Gemma tripped on her feet a bit trying to keep up.

"You need to turn his head," Cassie continued, not looking back at her sister's struggle.

"Turn his head?" Gemma was skeptical. "This is Tyler we're talking about."

Cassie opened the door to her bedroom, shutting it again once they were both inside. "It doesn't matter. It's still a first date. Sit."

She pointed to her bed. "I'm sure I can find a flattering, yet fitting, outfit for you to wear." She crossed to her closet and practically stuck her head inside as she searched through it.

Gemma pushed out a groan and dropped onto the blue-and-white patchwork quilt that Gram had made. It looked almost the same as the green one on her own bed. "This really isn't necessary. And Tyler's going to be here soon. I don't have time to change." She crossed her legs, resting her chin in her upturned hands.

Emerging from the closet, Cassie said, "Nonsense. This will only take a minute. I'll stall for you if he comes." No sooner had she said the words than her head disappeared into the clothes again. There was no stopping her when she got in makeover mode.

Gemma tried not to take it personally. Her own fashion sense would consist of sweats and athletic tees if it weren't for Cassie's frequent assistance. She'd asked for her help on more than one occasion when getting ready for a date. Especially a first date.

But this wasn't a typical first date. This was Tyler. She'd never dressed to impress him before, and she wasn't sure if she wanted to start now. They were already in an odd sort of limbo land—not exactly friends, but definitely not dating. What if emphasizing the fact that this was a date made their situation even more uncomfortable? She'd watched a few friends in college shift between friendship and more, only to realize they weren't compatible and go their separate ways. They'd never talked to each other again.

She didn't want that to happen with Tyler, not even after the roller coaster of emotions they'd been riding the last few weeks.

Cassie continued riffling through her closet. She pulled out a yellow, flowery crocheted tank top and studied it with squinty eyes. Then she shook her head, returned the top to the closet, and kept searching.

How many outfits did she bring? Gemma thought, though it shouldn't have surprised her. Cassie always had the most luggage whenever their family would travel home. Every potential occasion needed at least one outfit, but more likely two to account for mood changes. And there could never be any repeating clothing items. So different than Gemma's shove-all-your-things-in-a-backpack kind of packing style.

"I know I have something in here. What about this?" She pulled her head out of the closet again, holding a black, glitzy tank top that didn't look like it covered very much.

Panic crept up Gemma's spine. "I am not wearing that," she said adamantly.

Cassie studied it, then looked back at her sister. "Why not? I think it would be cute on you."

"It looks like something you'd wear to a nightclub. Not an early evening baseball game. One wrong move and it could fall right off."

Her sister put her pointer finger to her mouth in thought. "Hm ... maybe you're right." She replaced the top on the rack in the closet and kept looking.

After Gemma had rejected the next three outfits for various reasons—too sparkly, too tight, way too much pink—she could tell her sister was getting frustrated. Well, good. She was getting frustrated too. She was just about to put an end to the misery when Cassie reemerged from the closet.

"Ah ha!" she exclaimed with a look of triumph on her flawless face. She held out a mint-green sundress with tiny yellow and white flowers printed on the fabric and gave a decisive nod. "This color looks great on you." It wasn't the first time she'd mentioned that green was Gemma's best color. "And not a speck of pink anywhere on it."

Gemma eyed the sundress suspiciously. "It's a dress."

"Honestly, Gem," Cassie grumbled. "Would it kill you to wear a dress one time? If you pair it with some sensible sandals or cute canvas sneakers, it will totally be casual enough to look good but still be comfortable for what you're doing. And you'll look super cute in it."

Gemma highly doubted all of that. Comfort and dresses were two words she'd never put together. But she sighed and took it before rising from the bed, more than ready to put an end to this misery.

She appreciated her sister's help. Really, she did. And part of her loved seeing Cassie in her element. It wasn't a selfish endeavor either. Cassie had a natural way with people, and it was clear she loved helping them look their best. Would it really be so bad to wear a dress one time to make her sister happy?

"I'll wait downstairs," Cassie said as they exited the bedroom together, "in case he comes while you're getting dressed." She headed off toward the stairs.

Gemma pushed down the hesitation she felt over Cassie and Tyler being alone together as she went in the opposite direction toward the end of the hall. Once she was in her room, she surveyed herself in the full-length mirror behind the closed door, taking in her curly brown hair, then moved to the red-and-white baseball tee and shorts and finished with her well-loved tennis shoes.

A sinking feeling settled in her gut. She'd promised her teenage self she'd never change herself because of a guy again. Wearing this dress seemed like going against everything that girl had worked to overcome.

But as much as she hated to admit it, she did want to impress Tyler. She'd wanted that since the very first conversation they'd had while standing on opposite sides of the stucco wall between their houses when they were ten. Would wearing this dress do the trick? Maybe putting herself through a little discomfort was worth it if it helped him see her as more than one of the guys. Was it so wrong to want that?

She hurried out of her current outfit, tossing it on her bed before throwing the sundress over her head. The fabric felt light on her skin, the skirt flowy around her legs, the hem hitting at mid-thigh.

You need to turn his head, Cassie had said. This outfit would definitely do the trick. If she were being honest with herself, she did look kind of cute. And yet, the woman staring back at her didn't seem like her.

It's just one date, she thought, adjusting a few curls that had been displaced as she'd changed. Once the date was over, she could go back to her usual comfort clothes. She swallowed the disgust and walked back downstairs.

"Look at you!" Cassie squealed the moment she spotted her. "You're gorgeous! There's no way Tyler won't love you in that dress."

Gemma attempted a smile, though it felt more like a grimace. Cassie was too busy fussing over a stubborn curl that refused to cooperate to notice, chatting about something that Gemma didn't catch. Her heart was pounding too loudly in her ears to bother keeping up with the speed of Cassie's chatter.

She shifted her gaze to Gram, who was watching the whole interaction from the couch. Her grandmother didn't give anything away from her expression. Once Gemma's hair was declared perfect, she took a seat next to her.

"You look nice," Gram said simply.

Gemma chose to ignore the slight question in her grandmother's statement and took her hand. "Thanks. Are you doing okay?"

"I'm still here, so I guess that's something." Gram nodded, her mouth turning up a bit. "Apparently, it's not my time to go quite yet. Even if that makes your grandpa a little impatient."

Gemma gently kissed Gram's wrinkled cheek. "I'm sure he'll understand. We still need you here."

"Grandpa will just have to wait a little longer," Cassie said, perching on the arm of the couch on Gram's other side.

Gram smiled and reached for her hand. Cassie gave it to her without hesitation, glancing fondly back at her. Then Gram shifted her loving gaze to Gemma on her right. "It's so good to have both my granddaughters here with me."

Gemma leaned gently against her grandmother's side, careful not to put too much pressure on her bad wrist. Before long, her sister slid an arm around Gram's shoulders and began stroking Gemma's curls. It reminded Gemma of all the times they snuggled up together to watch TV or talk when they were young. Then Cassie had discovered boys and everything had changed. The gesture now was nice, connecting them in a way they hadn't for far too long.

They sat like that for a few moments, and for the first time in a while, Gemma's thoughts stilled. She couldn't help but think that maybe, just maybe, things were starting to look up. Gram was recovering, even if she still had a long way to go to be back to normal, whatever that new normal may be. Tyler had asked her out on a date, and amazingly, Cassie seemed to be encouraging it, which meant that Gemma had no reason to question her intentions. Perhaps moving past what happened seven years ago was still a possibility.

The buzzing of Cassie's phone interrupted the tender moment. She glanced at the screen and sighed. "I should take this," she said, sliding her hand back and rising from the couch. She hurried from the room.

What was that about? Gemma wondered, concern for her sister creeping into her mind. She ignored it, telling herself that Cassie would tell her if she wanted to and realizing that she had more than enough to worry about right now.

Gram placed a hand on Gemma's bare thigh. "I'm glad I have a few moments with you before your date. I expect Tyler will be here soon."

She was right. Any minute now, he'd knock on the door. Gemma squirmed in her seat, her nerves returning.

"Tyler is a lot like your grandpa," Gram continued, her words slow.

Gemma tried not to let her surprise show on her face. She hadn't noticed any resemblance between the two. Grandpa Will's hair had been white for as long as she'd known him, but she'd loved looking at black-and-white pictures of him in his younger years when it had been dark like hers and Dad's. Tyler was blond. And taller than her grandpa, if only by a few inches.

A faraway look appeared in Gram's eyes as if she were thinking about her lost love. "There is no such thing as a perfect man. Not even your father could make me want to pull my hair out as much as Grandpa did. But he was good to his very core. I could tell from the minute I met him that Tyler is the same."

Where was she going with this?

Gemma didn't speak her question out loud. Had her hesitation with him, and the uncertainty of the situation, been that obvious? She thought she'd done a better job at hiding it.

"However, my dear," Gram continued, "even he isn't worth changing who you are in order to catch his eye."

Shame washed over Gemma as her grandmother assessed her appearance, her eyes traveling up and down her torso multiple times. The sudden urge to disappear caught up with her, and she slumped deeper into the couch cushion. "Do you think I should change?"

Gram made a humming noise, neither agreeing nor disagreeing with Gemma's question. Instead, she said, "That choice is yours. I'm only saying what needs to be said."

Gemma blew out a breath. Gram was right. Why had she let Cassie talk her into this horrible outfit? It was cute but definitely not her.

"I'll go change." Gemma kissed her grandmother's cheek. "Thanks, Gram."

She stood, but before she'd gone more than a step, Gram spoke again. "Gemma?"

Gemma turned back.

"Don't be too hard on Cassie. She means well."

Gemma paused for a few seconds, unsure of how to respond. Was Gram referring to this ill-conceived outfit or something else entirely? How much did she know about what happened between them?

After a brief hesitation, Gemma nodded and continued toward the stairs. Unfortunately, she didn't even make it halfway up before a knock broke the silence in the entryway. Tyler's knock. The same one he'd used as a kid when he was hanging outside her window.

She froze. What should she do? Gram wasn't capable of getting to the door. And with her parents out of the house and Cassie on the phone, the task of letting Tyler in fell to Gemma.

With slow, reluctant steps, she headed back downstairs, pausing to compose herself. She breathed in deeply through her nose, closing her eyes, then let it out slowly through her mouth. Not quite ready, she did it again. After the third time, she pulled the door open.

Tyler stood on the doorstep, dressed in a USC T-shirt and matching baseball cap. "Whoa." He stepped back, brows darting up in surprise.

His eyes traveled down the front of her. Not in a disrespectful way—he seemed more confused than anything—but his scrutiny still made her want to shrink into herself.

"You look beautiful, Gem," he said. "Are you ready to go?"

She tried to act natural, like she'd intended this look all along. It was too late to change now. "Yeah, let's go." She grabbed the drawstring bag that held her wallet and phone from the floor by the door and stepped onto the porch.

Tyler placed a hand on the small of her back, a simple gesture inviting her to start walking. She resisted the urge to shiver. When they got to his Honda parked at the curb, he held the door open for her as she climbed in and tucked her skirt tightly around her legs. She used the time it took him to circle around to the driver's seat to let out a deep breath, easing her nerves.

"I'm really glad you agreed to come with me," he said once they were on their way. "With how much time we spent playing ball growing up, I don't think we've ever been to an actual game together. It seems wrong, you know?"

Gemma tugged on the strap of her dress, assuring the neckline gave her maximum coverage in the chest area. "You never went to any Chilean national games? My parents took me a couple times."

"We always talked about going," Tyler said, glancing briefly at her as she rearranged the skirt of her dress. Again. "But things kept getting in the way, and we never made it up that far north where they played. We did go to a few soccer games over the years, though that's nothing to brag about."

She paused in her effort to inconspicuously find a sitting position that wouldn't burn her skin to smirk at him. The leather of the seat was so hot, and her dress so short that no matter where she moved her legs, the fabric never quite covered enough to prevent the scorching.

"That's because it's soccer." She shuddered dramatically.

Tyler laughed at that. They stopped at the red light leading onto the freeway and he tossed her a wink. His humor faded when he noticed her fidgeting. Confusion once again pulled at his features as he watched her. "Is something wrong?"

Busted. She froze, then slowly turned to him. "I'm fine?" Why did that sound like a question? "Why?"

He pursed his lips, clearly not convinced. "It just seems like you're uncomfortable right now. Is something wrong with your clothes? Are you hot? I know the seats can get a little warm when the car has been parked in the sun for a while." His expression turned uncertain. "It's not … me, is it?"

When did he develop such a keen sense of observation? During their six years of friendship, it almost took Gemma beating him over the head with a club to get him to pick up on subtle cues. She wasn't sure she liked this new personality trait.

She debated whether to confess what was really bothering her. There wasn't anything she could do about her outfit now. On the other hand, she was in for a very miserable date if she had to hide her discomfort for the entire game.

"Yes …" She shook her head, still unsure how to answer. "I mean no." Her shoulders slumped, and she sighed. "It's the dress. Cassie wanted me to wear it to impress you. But I hate it. It's just not … me."

Tyler didn't answer right away. Didn't even look at her. Was he confused? Disappointed that Gemma wasn't the feminine woman he wanted her to be?

"Why did you think you had to dress a certain way to impress me?" he finally asked quietly, not taking his eyes off the road.

She stared at her hands balled together in her lap. "I'm not ready to answer that question." Giving him a reason—*the* reason—would mean sharing her true feelings, opening herself up to more pain. Sure, he'd asked her on a date, but that could mean anything.

Before she knew what was happening, Tyler reached over and set his hand on top of her knee. Her skin tingled at his touch. "Gem, let me be perfectly clear. I think you look amazing right now." He stole a quick glance at her to make sure she was listening.

She was listening. She was hanging onto his every word.

"But it's not what you're wearing that impresses me," he continued, finding her hand and giving it a squeeze. "I really don't care what you have on. It's *you* who impresses me." The traffic ahead slowed to a stop, and Tyler did as well. He used the opportunity to turn his attention to her. "You're my favorite person in the entire world. You always have been. And I suspect you always will be."

His words filled her with warmth. No one had ever said anything like that to her before. Soaking in the intensity of his gaze, and that irresistible half smile, she knew he was telling the truth.

The traffic started moving again, and he removed his hand from hers, returning it to the wheel. Gemma relaxed in her seat, feeling more comfortable than she had since he'd picked her up for this date. Their conversation soon moved away from her outfit to other topics for the rest of the drive. When they arrived on campus, Tyler showed his expertise in all things USC baseball by finding a parking spot a short walk from the stadium.

"I'm impressed," Gemma admitted out loud as he maneuvered the car into a tight spot behind a beat-up pickup truck and in front of a silver sedan.

He chuckled. "With my parking abilities? My skill is pretty amazing, isn't it?"

She gave him a wry smile. "That too. But I was talking more about the location."

"Ah, that. The early bird gets the worm, as they say. When you've been to as many games as I have, you know all the best spots to park."

As they joined the group of spectators heading toward the front gates—most of them decked out from head to toe in cardinal and gold—Gemma stood out like a sore thumb in her dress. They certainly looked a lot more comfortable in their jerseys and face paint than she did, and she wished for at least the hundredth time that she hadn't let Cassie talk her into changing her outfit. Her conversation with Tyler in the car had helped, but no amount of words of affirmation would change her hatred of wearing a dress.

Tyler handed his phone to the attendant to scan their tickets and they entered the stadium. They approached their section near the first base side, and Gemma spotted a stand just past the entrance exploding with all kinds of baseball paraphernalia. Jerseys and athletic tees shared the space with both small and large white plush horses wearing gold saddles. There were baseball hats and helmets and all the classic game snacks.

An idea struck her. "Where are our seats?" she asked, turning to Tyler.

He held his phone out to her, the tickets still up on the screen. "Just in there," he said, pointing to their gate. "Why?"

Gemma committed the row and seat numbers to memory. "I need to do something. I'll meet you down there?"

Tyler's eyes scrunched slightly, and his mouth opened like he was about to ask. But then he shut it again and swallowed. "Okay. I'll see you soon."

Gemma waited until he'd disappeared through the gate before continuing toward the merchandise stand.

Chapter Twenty-Two

Where is she?

Tyler checked the clock on his phone before turning around in his seat to scan the top of the stairs. Almost twenty minutes had passed since he'd left Gemma at the entrance to their gate. The national anthem had already been sung by a local a cappella group and the Trojans were on the field, wrapping up their final warmup. If she didn't hurry, she'd miss the first pitch.

Opening their latest text thread, he typed out a quick message.

Tyler: Everything OK?

No response came. All around him, the crowd on the first base side was growing rapidly as more fans found their seats. Tyler picked up on snippets of conversation from the people near him as he turned to face the field again. Adjusting his leg out in front of him, his shoe landed on a sticky spot on the pavement.

The music bouncing around the stadium cut out, and a voice came over the loudspeaker, announcing the first batter. A few cheers rang out from the spectators around him. He checked his phone again.

Still no sign of Gemma.

What could she possibly be doing that would take her so long? Had she gotten lost? Maybe he should go find her.

No sooner had he made up his mind to do that did he turn around in his seat as a group of fans came down the stairs, their cardinal and gold outfits putting his single T-shirt and baseball cap to shame. One even wore a floppy gold hat that looked like it had come straight out of a Dr. Seuss book.

He was so preoccupied with the group that it took a minute to realize that Gemma had slipped into the seat next to him. She plopped a plate of nachos onto his lap. The green sundress she'd had on when they'd arrived was nowhere in sight. She'd replaced it with a cardinal shirt with gold lettering and black athletic shorts.

What did she do with the dress? He eyed the small drawstring bag at her feet, and his silent question was answered.

"I hope you know how much it pains me to be wearing this right now," she said, rolling her eyes at him.

Tyler laughed, remembering the many times they'd played up their division rivalry as kids. He'd given her a hard time when she'd cheered for Oregon. And she'd dished it right back to him. "That's too bad. You'll have to get used to it now that you live down here. It's time to put away your Oregon loyalties."

She gasped, bringing a hand to her chest. "Blasphemy! You'll never get me to come over to the dark side."

He shook his head slowly, clucking his tongue. "If only it worked like that. My powers of persuasion are very strong."

She snorted. "I'd like to see how strong they are once you leave LA."

Oh yeah. That did put a damper on things. But he wasn't moving up north until July. Three months should be enough time to win her over. At least that was the hope.

He leaned closer to whisper in her ear. "You have no idea how strong they can be." She shivered, and he sat back, unable to keep the grin of satisfaction off his face. She might try hard to act like she wasn't interested in him, but that reaction told a different story.

Sliding his hat off his head, he placed it on hers as if he were carrying out some sort of coronation. "I now declare you officially one of us."

He dragged his eyes over her, stealing a good look. His heart thumped hard. It seemed to be performing complicated backflips in his chest.

What. The. Heck.

It was a hat. A crown of cotton-polyester fabric with a bill extending from the front. He'd seen her wear dozens over the years. Possibly even hundreds. So why was seeing her in his right now doing such weird things to him?

Granted, her outfit now was by far his favorite of her "looks." It was the look that made her the most comfortable. That wasn't to say she wasn't beautiful in that green sundress she'd had on earlier.

No, beautiful wasn't a strong enough word. Stunning was a more accurate description. Although he hadn't done a very good job at hiding his surprise to see her in it. He knew she hated dresses. She'd always gone to great lengths to avoid them, so the fact that she'd put one on for him was touching, but completely unnecessary.

Why did she feel the need to impress him anyway? Her answer when he'd asked exactly that was just as puzzling as her choice of outfit. *I'm not ready to answer that question,* she'd said. What did that even mean?

"Technically, that's not true until I start my graduate program this fall," Gemma said.

Tyler blinked. What wasn't true? What were they even talking about?

She seemed to pick up on his confusion. "You said I was one of you now. Except I refuse to cheer for your team when they're playing the Ducks. I'll proudly wear my yellow and green, even if I'm the only one in the stadium."

That's right. They were talking about sports. Definitely not how gorgeous she looked in a dress. A strange laugh pushed its way out of him, much too forceful to come even close to natural. He cleared his throat. "Fair enough. And I promise not to pretend I don't know you."

Gemma tossed him a teasing smile, pulling one out of him as well. When an increase of cheers rang out around them, he turned his attention back to the field only to realize they'd missed the entire first half of the inning. It was just as well. The game was already more interesting with her sitting next to him.

Gemma reached over to pluck a tortilla chip from the tray of nachos in Tyler's lap. She scooped a generous amount of cheese onto it. "What is it that makes these nachos so amazing? I mean, they're just chips and cheese from a jar. Nothing special. And yet, they're so good." She bit off half of it, then stuffed the rest into her mouth when it crumbled in her fingers.

He picked up a chip already smothered in cheese. "It wouldn't be a baseball game without chips and fake cheese." He crunched down on the whole thing in a way that would have Mom cringing at his lack of manners. "Mmmm, tasty," he mumbled through a mouth full of food.

She laughed, the lightness of it carrying over the constant commotion of the crowd. He glanced at her as she turned her head to him, and their eyes met. He winked, pulling a carefree smile from her. She used to grin at him like that all the time when they were kids. It didn't have quite the same effect on him back then though. Now that his feelings for her ran so much deeper, it felt like he'd won the lottery.

Suddenly, and without warning, she reached a hand to his cheek, brushing her fingers against his jawline. Tyler froze, his breath catching in his throat. He swallowed slowly.

"You have cheese on your face," she said, holding up her hand to show him the smudge of orange on her pointer finger.

They'd once been so close that something as simple as wiping food off his face wouldn't have been a big deal. Now, that little gesture sent his mind swirling into a void that only involved Gemma Schalk's touch on his jaw, not whatever was happening on the field in front of them.

Game? What game?

She met his eyes, and something in his gaze must have caught her attention because she didn't look away. The commotion around them faded to a low buzz as they watched each other. Tyler had to clamp down on the desire to kiss her right then and there.

We're in public, he reminded himself. And yet, the need to finally kiss her wouldn't be appeased unless he followed through with it. Why did these instincts creep up at the worst times?

Maybe one little kiss wouldn't hurt. He leaned toward her, catching her eye. She didn't move closer, but she didn't pull away either.

"Heads up!"

The voice from behind them sounded a lot closer than it should have. A second later, a baseball glove reached over them to snag a foul ball that almost clocked Tyler right in the head. Cheers echoed through the stands from the people around them.

"That was a concussion waiting to happen." The guy who'd caught the ball smirked at him as if he knew exactly what Tyler had been about to do. "Try paying more attention to the game instead of making googly eyes at your sweetheart, here, huh?" he said, his jaw working overtime on a large wad of chewing gum. He waggled his bushy eyebrows.

Tyler ground his teeth. "I'll keep that in mind," he muttered under his breath.

He caught Gemma's expression as he turned back around. Her cheeks glowed a deep red, and she had her eyes squeezed shut. And although her lips were pursed like she was trying not to laugh, her shoulders shook with the unsuccessful effort.

He bumped her arm with his to get her attention. That only managed to break the dam of her not-so-carefully-controlled composure. A laugh burst from her, causing Tyler to break out in the biggest grin of his life.

"You should pay more attention to the game, Ty," she teased, bumping him back. "You might miss something important."

Nothing is more important than you. He was tempted to say it out loud, but he didn't need any more flak from the machismo behind them.

"Good thing the nachos are safe," he said instead, plucking a chip from the tray that had shifted a bit between them during the commotion.

"Phew!" Gemma slid a hand across her forehead as she said it, a twinkle in her eye. "We don't want ruined nachos, do we?" She turned back to watch the action on the field.

Tyler had a harder time pulling his attention away from her. For perhaps the first time in his life, he didn't care one bit what was happening in the game. His entire focus was on the beautiful woman beside him.

It wasn't the angry roar of the crowd a minute later that snapped him from his daze. Instead, it was Gemma, cupping her hands around her mouth and yelling at the umpire. "Come on, ump. You call that a strike? It was way outside the box!"

Here was the Gemma Schalk of his childhood, heckling the umpire like she'd heckled whatever neighborhood boys had made up the opposing team when they'd played in the grassy field near their homes in Santiago. If he had known that one baseball game would bring out the best friend he'd known and loved growing up, he would've taken her to one weeks ago.

Loved.

There was that word again. The impact of it hit him like that dumb train problem he always got wrong in math class. If Train A left San Francisco at eight a.m. going fifty miles per hour, and Train B left New York at eight p.m. going sixty miles per hour, what time would they collide with Tyler's heart? He still didn't know how to solve the problem, but he knew the correct answer.

Right now. That was the answer.

Gemma Schalk was no longer simply his childhood playmate. Or the person he was developing feelings for. She was his person. The one who completed him in a way that no other woman had. Perhaps she always had been, and he'd just never realized it. But he was keenly aware of it now.

He loved her. And not in a best friend kind of way. He loved all of her, as a woman, a friend, and the person his heart wanted with him always.

Reaching over, he snagged her hand in his. She turned to him, her brows shooting up in surprise, though she didn't pull away. She offered him a small smile before turning back to the game.

With their fingers still tangled together, Tyler knew their friendship had just changed again. Only time would tell what happened next.

Chapter Twenty-Three

"You seemed to enjoy yourself tonight," Tyler said when they arrived back at Gemma's house after the game.

"I did." She swung their connected hands back and forth as they walked up the path to the front door. She still couldn't believe she was holding his hand. And not in a buddy-buddy kind of way. More like an I-like-you kind of way. "I really did. Thanks for inviting me."

They stopped underneath the porch awning. She turned to face him, wrapping her free arm around her middle for warmth.

"Are you cold?" he asked.

She lifted her shoulders. "A little." Served her right for starting out the evening in such a lightweight dress. It was now crumpled at the bottom of the drawstring bag on her back—Cassie wouldn't be too happy about that—but Gemma wished she'd had the foresight to splurge for a sweatshirt too. The thought had crossed her mind until she remembered that she still didn't have a job. Now that her parents were here, she determined to put finding one higher on her priority list.

Tyler set his arms around her, pulling her in close to him as if it were the most natural thing in the world. And perhaps it was. For him at least. A thrill zipped through her all the same.

"I never thought I'd see the day you cheered for the Trojans," he said through a chuckle. He placed his hands on her upper arms and started rubbing up and down, the friction causing delightful waves of heat sparking through her extremities. "Should I start preparing for the apocalypse now?"

She scrunched her nose at him in amusement. "The end of the world is coming, Ty. You better break out your survival kit."

"I still can't believe you heckled that umpire." His smile grew, exposing the small dimple in his left cheek. "I mean, I probably should have expected it after all those times you taunted Peter every time you struck him out, but I didn't see it coming tonight."

"I'm full of surprises, aren't I?" She gave him a coy smile as she backed up out of his hold. Grabbing his hand again, she tugged him toward the swing, an unspoken invitation for him to stay a little longer. He accepted it, and soon they were comfortably situated on the cushions. Gemma sat sideways with one knee bent against the back of the seat, and he angled his body slightly to face her, rocking the swing gently back and forth with his foot.

"I like it," he said, placing his hand on the thigh of her leg hanging off the swing, sliding it barely underneath the hem of her shorts. "It keeps things interesting."

The urge to shiver came over her again. This time it wasn't from the cold. She managed to hold it back as she dropped her hand on top of his and locked their fingers together.

Tyler's focus shifted to their interlocked hands, and he swallowed. "Listen, Gem. There's something I haven't been able to stop thinking about." His voice was soft, hesitant.

She watched his eyes slowly—agonizingly slowly—travel up to meet hers. Anticipation crackled in the air between them. She had a pretty good idea of what the *something* was without him even saying it. She couldn't stop thinking about their almost kiss too.

"What is it?" she asked anyway.

He cleared his throat and opened his mouth to speak. Then closed it again. The anticipation was killing her. Was he going to tell her it was a mistake? Apologize for it? Say he wanted to do it again? She wanted to scream at him to spit it out, or better yet, take matters into her own hands—or lips, as the case may be—and kiss him herself.

"About the other day, when we almost ... you know." He stopped again.

"When we almost kissed," she prompted in a whisper, staring at the gold lettering on his T-shirt as her cheeks warmed. When she returned her attention to his face, he was watching her, his eyes dancing between hers and her lips.

"Yeah, that." His gaze pierced her soul, daring her to plunge even deeper into the unknown territory between friendship and more. "The thing is"—his voice dropped to a whisper—"I regret that I didn't actually get to kiss you."

Gemma's breath caught. Before she could come up with a response, Tyler was sliding one hand behind her neck, pulling her closer. All the air whooshed out of her in a small gasp seconds before his lips brushed against hers. It was a whisper of a kiss, as if he were testing the water to check if it was warm enough to swim.

Yep, definitely warm enough. She tangled her fingers through his blond hair, an invitation to dive in for more.

He did.

Fireworks exploded in her mind like the finale of an epic Fourth of July show. With each caress of their lips, she clung to him tighter, afraid if she let go, this would all be a dream.

If this was a dream, she didn't ever want to wake up. Kissing him surpassed even the most exquisite dreams she'd had of this moment. She never realized it could feel like this, affecting every inch of her body and soul.

"Gemma," Tyler murmured on an exhale when he broke off to take a breath. That's all he said, as though even her name alone was sacred.

A dizzy sensation danced around her head, and before she could catch her own breath, he was back for more, deepening his affections and the connection between them. Tyler's hand slid up her thigh to wrap around her waist, tugging her closer, closer, and closer until the small distance that still existed between them disappeared.

Out of nowhere, the image of Tyler holding her sister exactly this way collided with her current reality. *Is this how he kissed Cassie?*

And just like that, the proverbial lake dried up. The fireworks fizzled out. All the euphoria of the moment vanished in midair, and Gemma gasped.

Tyler picked up on the change in energy immediately. "What is it?"

She slid away from him, finding a home on the opposite side of the bench. "I'm ... uh ..." What was she supposed to say? For years she'd dreamed of being able to kiss him like that. Dreamed of the day he'd realize she was his person. And now that it was here, her insecurities had to creep in and ruin everything.

She wanted a relationship with him. More now than ever after tonight. But how was she supposed to move forward with him if every time they kissed, she pictured him with Cassie?

"I'm sorry," she said, swiping at her cheek with the back of her hand. "I don't think I can do this."

He scooted to her side but kept a healthy distance between them. "No, I'm sorry. I guess I read the signs wrong. I thought this was what you wanted."

She shook her head vigorously. The tears fell faster, now traveling down both cheeks. "No. You didn't. I'm just so ..." She forced herself to look at him, his handsome face blurry through the moisture in her eyes.

"Gem, please talk to me," he pleaded, reaching for her hand and sandwiching it in both of his. "Something tells me this has more to do than me being a bad kisser."

A tiny laugh hiccuped from her. "It's not that."

Definitely not that. She'd probably never experience a kiss like his ever again.

Her shoulders dropped as she slumped against the back of the swing. She pushed out a heavy sigh. "I don't know what's wrong with me. I should be really happy right now. You told me earlier that I'm your favorite person and that you regret not kissing me the other day. Your actions are telling me that you have feelings for me, and then you go and kiss me like that ... I should want this. I *do* want this."

"Then what's the problem?"

She dropped her head. "I don't think I can be in a relationship with a guy who has also made out with my sister."

Now it was his turn to blow out a heavy breath. "So you do know about that."

She refused to look at him as she nodded.

"Did Cassie tell you?" His tone wasn't accusatory, nor did it seem to hold any regret. It sounded more curious than anything.

So that's how it was going to be? Wasn't he at least a little bit sorry about it? "She didn't need to. I saw it myself." That sounded like she'd intentionally spied on them, so she hurried to explain. "I'd been trying to go to sleep, but the house was too loud, so I decided to get some fresh air. When I came around the house to the backyard, I saw the two of you on the bench, and I ..." He got the picture.

At first, he didn't react. Then he took back his hand and folded it with his other in his lap. "That's why you wouldn't say goodbye." It wasn't a question. "You were avoiding me."

"That night was humiliating for me." Did he really not get it? Why did she have to spell it out for him? "First, you all but referred to me as your sister—"

"I did?" He cocked his head, squinting one eye in his confusion. "I don't remember saying that."

She used to find his squinty eye quirk adorable when they were kids, but it only agitated her more right then. "Well, I do. And trust me, that was bad enough without walking in on you and my sister making out." She squeezed her eyes shut against the image that was starting to make itself comfy in her memory. There it was again, playing like a movie on the insides of her eyelids. She snapped them open again.

Tyler was silent for a few beats. Then, in a resigned voice, he said, "Gemma—"

She held up a hand. "I don't need to hear your excuses."

"You don't even know what I was going to say." A hint of frustration leaked through his words.

"Nothing you say would change what happened." She had half a mind to go inside and leave him out here on his own to wallow in what he did. Except her legs had locked up and wouldn't move. Instead, she crossed her arms over her stomach to guard herself against whatever came next.

Apparently, he wasn't planning on holding back. "That was seven years ago." He spoke quietly. "It happened one time, and we never talked again after that. Honest. It didn't mean anything."

Well, that was a gut punch if Gemma ever felt one. "That kind of makes it worse, don't you think? I'd expect Cassie to act like that, but I didn't think you were the kind of guy to kiss and run. And I don't want to date someone like that."

Something fierce flashed in Tyler's usually kind eyes. "So, you're judging the man I am now by something I did when I was young and stupid? That hardly seems fair. Why does it even matter if I have feelings for you now?"

"Because I loved you!" Gemma choked out through more tears. "I always loved you. And you didn't even realize it. Do you know how hurtful that was?"

Tyler's eyebrows shot up. "Gemma—"

"I'm not done," she said over him. His mouth snapped closed. "These feelings might be new for you, but they're not for me. I didn't want to risk ruining our friendship, so I kept them inside, hoping you'd come around eventually and realize you loved me too. But why would you? I'm just one of the guys. That's all I've ever been to you."

She stood up so quickly that it caught him off guard, and the swing shot back. Before he could move out of its path, it swung forward again, hitting Gemma's calves. Her knees buckled under her, and she fell back against the swing.

Face burning, she stood again, more carefully this time. "Thank you for the date, but I'm ready to call it a night." She marched toward the door.

"Gemma," he called after her, a lot calmer than she would expect after that conversation.

At the door, she stopped, giving him a passing glance over her shoulder. "Please don't call me. I need some space to think."

In a scene slightly resembling a couple weeks before, she left him baffled on her porch while she went into the house, slamming the door behind her.

Chapter Twenty-Four

I've always loved you.

Tyler was still in shock over Gemma's confession, even as he arrived home after work the next day. She'd been in love with him all along? How had he missed that? He knew he could be a bit dense at times, but he should've spotted at least some clues if she'd really had feelings for him. He didn't think she was that good at hiding things. What other secrets had he not picked up on?

He rubbed his eyes, trying to clear away the stinging fatigue. Sleep had been a fickle friend last night. His mind kept replaying his whole conversation with Gemma—and the way she'd screamed the words in her frustration—over and over like a police detective going through video evidence of a crime. Each time, it ended at the same place. *I've always loved you.*

Stop. Rewind. Repeat.

This whole time he'd believed that once he figured out what had caused her to ghost him in the first place, he'd be able to fix the issue.

But how was he supposed to fix a kiss?

Tyler pushed down the guilt. *I didn't know*, he reminded himself, a tiny amount of indignation creeping its way past the regret. They weren't dating back then. He wasn't even sure they were dating now. Did he really deserve to be punished for a crime when he didn't know it was one?

He entered the kitchen, only to be greeted by a disgruntled Brad complaining to Tyler's sisters and Kendall. "Of course *my* sister would be the one to bring a date to a family dinner," he grumbled, slamming the refrigerator door shut, a 2-liter bottle of soda in his hand.

"What's the big deal?" Hallie asked, setting plates and utensils on the kitchen island. "We're all friends here. The more, the merrier."

Brad shot a scowl in her direction, then flicked his head up to Tyler in greeting. "Hey, man."

Tyler flashed an unenthusiastic two-fingered salute and sank onto one of the stools as his cousin resumed the conversation.

"Don't you think it's too soon to meet the family? They've been on one date. And I'm hungry."

Ah, therein lay the real issue. Brad wasn't bothered that Beej was bringing a guy. He was used to his sister's dating habits, after all. And this wasn't an official family dinner. Those happened on Sundays. The girls often came over a few times a week to hang out. They said it was because of the bigger kitchen, but they usually ended up ordering takeout anyway. Go figure.

Kendall picked up her phone from where it was charging on the counter by the swinging door. "She just texted me. They've picked up dinner and will be here soon. Do you think your stomach will survive? Or are you about to collapse on the floor in hunger right now? Because I'd actually like to see that."

"Ha," Brad grunted, making a face at her. "Good one."

"To be honest," Elise began, turning off the faucet so she could be heard. She set the glass she was filling with water on the counter next to her and looked at Tyler. "I'm kind of surprised you didn't invite Gemma to join us. You two are getting kind of cozy, aren't you?"

Oh, great. She had to bring up the one topic he did *not* want to talk about. As he searched for a way to sidestep this conversation, he caught Brad's knowing smirk.

If you say something, I'll wipe that smug look right off your face. That was the threat Tyler hoped he communicated with the look he directed at his cousin.

Unfortunately, Brad either didn't catch his silent pleading, didn't understand the message, or chose to flat out ignore it. Probably the third option. That jerk.

"Oh, they're more than cozy now," he said. "Tyler's in *love*."

"Ooooh," Hallie and Elise crooned in unison.

"Please don't make a big deal out of it. Can't we talk about *anything* else?" Tyler asked a bit more desperately than he'd intended. He turned to the kitchen door, hoping that Beej would miraculously show up with her date. Meeting Mr. Right Now would surely distract them all from this conversation, wouldn't it?

Elise, water glass in hand, made herself comfy at the kitchen island. "It's not too late to call her. Maybe she hasn't eaten yet."

"Um ..." Tyler looked down at his hands, finding sudden interest in the small paper cut on his right pointer finger. There'd be no avoiding this topic now that his sisters were involved. "She asked for space. So, I'm giving it to her."

"Uh-oh." Hallie plopped down on a stool next to Elise. "That doesn't sound good."

"What did you do?" Kendall asked, right on par with her usual assumption that the guy was always wrong.

He wasn't in the wrong this time.

Or was he?

Tyler bit his bottom lip. "Well ... I kind of ..." He cleared his throat, then muttered, "... kissed her sister."

"You *what?*" All three women gaped at him with matching looks of horror.

Brad barked out a surprised laugh, almost falling off his stool with the force of it. "Wait, how'd you kiss her? Was it a little peck on the cheek like the way you'd kiss Grandma, or were you aiming for her tonsils?"

Tyler glared at him. "Not. Helping," he said through clenched teeth.

"You both are idiots." Kendall scoffed in disgust.

"You know I love you, Ty," Elise said, her tone understanding, though the slight edge in her voice told him she was trying very hard to keep it that way. "And you know I will stand by you until the end of the world. But I have to agree with Kendall on this one. What were you thinking?"

He threw up his hands. "Gee, I don't know. Let me step into my time machine and travel back to the night before we left Chile. Then I'd be able to tell you exactly what I was thinking." Which was probably not much, if he were being truthful.

"Wait." Her tone lifted immediately. "This happened in Chile? Oh, I thought you were talking recently. And she's been holding onto this for that long?"

Tyler heaved out a heavy breath. "Yeah. Apparently, she was in love with me."

"And you didn't know?" Hallie asked.

He blinked at her a few times before answering. "Obviously not. If I had, I'd like to think I would've had enough common sense not to kiss her sister."

"Doubtful," Kendall muttered. Then louder, she said, "Isn't there some kind of guy code that forbids you from kissing your best friend's sister? I'd think the repercussions would be even more egregious for you considering your best friend was, in fact, a girl." She snorted but tried to cover it up by clearing her throat.

Tyler rolled his eyes. "Sure, laugh it up, Chuckles. I admit that maybe it wasn't the best decision I've ever made in my life. But she'd never shown any hints about having feelings for me. Not once. Cassie tried to kiss me, I was curious, so I kissed her back. Is that really so wrong?"

"I, for one, don't see a problem with that," Brad conceded with a nod.

Hallie threw a perplexed look his way before addressing her brother. "I can see your point. But I can also understand her side as well. For a sixteen-year-old girl, seeing the boy you like kiss anyone else is enough to ruin your life. It would be even harder if that girl were her sister, especially her twin."

She may as well have kicked him in the groin. He hadn't thought about it that way. Since talking with Gemma the night before, he'd forced the initial guilt over hurting her out of the way to fight for his own innocence. What kind of best friend does that? Kendall was right. He *was* the idiot.

"So, what should I do?" he asked, hanging his head. "She told me not to call her. And the last time she needed space, she disappeared for seven years."

Kendall shook her head with pity. "Just say goodbye to any chance of dating her. There's no coming back from this."

"Thank you for the vote of confidence." Tyler slouched lower on the stool. "Does anyone have any helpful ideas?"

Just then, a quick knock came from the front door before it opened with a long squeak. "Hey, we're here!"

"Finally," Brad groaned, hopping up from his stool. "Beej, get in here! We're starving!"

As everyone began to file out of the kitchen, Hallie stopped Tyler with a hand on his arm.

"Don't listen to Kendall," she said when he faced her. They were now the only two in the kitchen. Voices carried to them from the entryway, assuring them that their conversation wouldn't be overheard. "You know how she is."

He nodded, waiting for her to continue.

"You can't beat yourself up over this. True, kissing your best friend's sister was a pretty bonehead move, even for a sixteen-year-old." She raised an eyebrow at him, and if it weren't for the teasing uptick of her mouth, her expression would have rivaled *the look* Mom gave him every time he got caught misbehaving.

He puffed out a reluctant laugh. "You don't have to tell me that. I already feel bad. Worse, actually, after that butt whooping Kendall gave me just now."

Hallie gave him a sympathetic smile. "The point I'm trying to make is that everyone makes mistakes. And you're one of the good guys. Deep down, with how close you and Gemma were before and how much you've been there for her recently, I'm sure she already knows that. Eventually, she'll remember it. Don't lose hope."

He bumped her gently with his hip. "Thanks, Hal. That means a lot."

Hallie shrugged and accepted his one-armed hug. "I'm here for you. You're a pretty good big brother, even if you are a little dense sometimes."

"And you're not always annoying for a little sister." Tyler laughed as he dodged her attempt to slug his arm, exiting the kitchen to join the others in the entryway.

Don't lose hope. It would take more than not losing hope to fix things with Gemma. She seemed to believe that he thought of her as one of the guys. She'd told him as much last night. And maybe that was true when they were kids. But it sure wasn't now. His heart had finally discovered what his eyes had failed to recognize before, and now it was up to him to prove that to her.

If only she'd give him the chance to try.

Chapter Twenty-Five

Being dateless on a Friday night never used to bother Gemma. In fact, she'd spent many weekend nights closing out the library on campus, studying until the lights turned off and they'd kicked her out. But hey, her perfect GPA didn't just happen out of nowhere.

For maybe the first time in her life, not having anywhere to be bothered her. That she could've spent the evening with Tyler if she hadn't blown up their friendship—for the third time—bothered her even more.

Just talk to him, she thought as she sat on her bed, squeezing the pillow between her arms. *Tell him you're sorry.*

She eyed her phone, barely visible from the top of her mahogany dresser, at war with herself. It really hurt that he hadn't realized why his kiss with Cassie bothered her. But something he'd said continued to stick with her even two days after the fact.

You're judging the man I am now by something I did when I was young and stupid? That hardly seems fair.

He was right. It wasn't fair. And yet, her pesky insecurities wouldn't drop the issue.

A quiet knock came from her bedroom door. A second later, it opened, and Cassie poked her head into the room. "Can I come in?"

"Sure." Gemma tossed the pillow to the side as her sister joined her on the bed. "What's up?"

"I should ask you the same question."

When she didn't respond, Cassie considered her for a moment with her head tilted to one shoulder. The way she seemed to be debating whether to say something made Gemma nervous.

"Are you okay?" Cassie asked. "My twinepathy is telling me you're fighting with yourself over something."

Gemma snorted. "Twinepathy?"

"It's a combination of twin and telepathy," her sister explained with a shrug.

"I got that, thanks."

Cassie flicked a perfect golden curl off her shoulder. "Anyway, did you and Tyler have a fight? You haven't been yourself since the game."

Gemma hadn't been herself since she'd moved to Buena Hills and discovered the guy she'd ghosted all those years ago lived on the other side of town. "Actually ..." Her stomach bubbled at the concern in her sister's eyes. "Can I ... ask you something?"

"Of course. You know you can talk to me about anything."

Well, not anything. It had taken seven years for this conversation to occur, and Gemma wasn't sure if she even wanted to have it now. Except letting go of her anger and hurt surrounding "the event" on her own obviously wasn't going to happen. She'd buried it, run from it, examined it to death, but she'd never worked through it. And she doubted she ever would without confronting her sister.

"The night before the Abernathys moved away—" She stopped and took a breath. "—did Tyler kiss you, or did you kiss him?"

Cassie's eyebrows shot up. "Did he tell you about that?" Her tone wasn't defensive. On the contrary, it sounded regretful. "I'm not surprised."

Gemma shook her head. "He didn't need to. I saw it myself."

Her sister looked down at her hands fiddling between her criss-crossed legs. Gemma held her breath waiting for the answer.

"It was me," Cassie said softly. The regret in her expression when she finally glanced up again was unmistakable.

Gemma brought her legs up to her chest and hugged her arms around them, clamping down on her jaw to keep her feelings from showing on her face. She needed answers, and she couldn't let the hurt prevent her from getting them. "But ... why? You had every guy in the neighborhood lining up to go out with you. Why did you have to have Tyler too?"

She expected Cassie to defend her actions, so the words she said took Gemma by surprise. "I'm really sorry. I never meant to hurt you. I had no idea you had feelings for him. You hid it so well from everyone."

"I didn't want him to know." Gemma spoke to her hands, the embarrassment washing over her as strongly as it had the night the kiss happened. "I was so afraid he wouldn't feel the same." She sniffed. "And I was right."

Cassie paused for a moment before she spoke. "I did a lot of things as a kid I wish I hadn't."

"Like what?" Her sister had grown a lot in the last few years, but Gemma hadn't realized she had regrets.

Cassie lifted her shoulders. "Like caring more about what boys thought of me than what I thought about myself." She leaned forward, an intensity in her movement as she grabbed Gemma's hands. "But one thing I won't ever regret is having you in my life. You're my sister. My favorite relationship. And if I'd known you liked Tyler as more than a friend, I never would have kissed him. I wouldn't dream of doing anything to intentionally hurt you."

Gemma kept her eyes on their hands. What was she supposed to say to that?

"Do you still have feelings for him?"

Not trusting herself to speak, Gemma simply nodded. A lump was forming in her throat, so she took a few breaths and swallowed, attempting to force it back down.

"I don't think I ever stopped," she whispered.

Her sister didn't give any reaction to her words, instead allowing Gemma to force out her confession at her own pace.

"That night was the worst night of my life," she continued. "I was finally going to tell him how I felt, but he made it very clear I was only a friend. And then I saw you two together ..." She shook her head to clear the mental image. "That's when I realized I'd never be the girl for him."

A small gasp escaped Cassie. "Gem, that's not true. Ever since

I've been here, I've watched you two together. Do you know what I see?"

"What?" Gemma asked, curiosity mixed with wariness in her tone.

Cassie's smile turned soft. "I see a guy who looks at you like you're the only person in the room." At Gemma's doubtful expression, her sister laughed. "No, seriously. When you're around, it's like no one else matters. Why do you think he does all those things for Gram?"

"Because he's a thoughtful guy," Gemma answered. "He's always been that way. His mom trained him well."

Cassie shrugged. "Well, yeah. That's true. But really, he's doing them because he knows how much Gram means to you. He's doing all of it *for you.*"

At her words, Gemma looked up. Was Cassie right? She thought about everything Tyler had done in the last few weeks. Dropping everything to come to the hospital after Gram's stroke. Visiting them every day, despite his busy class load and work schedule. Picking up her parents so she wouldn't have to leave Gram alone. The swing. Even something as little as bringing her a chocolate bar because he knew it was her favorite.

He'd been more solicitous in the last couple of weeks than Blake had been in their entire eighteen-month relationship. And all this time she'd responded with questions and doubts and insecurities.

And that kiss. Oh boy, that kiss. When she wasn't wallowing in the shame of once again pushing Tyler away, there were moments when she allowed herself to wander up to cloud nine because of it. Only briefly. Then reality would set in once again.

She touched the tip of her pointer finger to her lips. "He kissed me." She hadn't meant to admit the words out loud, but they escaped before she could stop them.

"Really?" The eagerness in Cassie's tone was impossible to miss.

"It was ..." Gemma didn't know why she suddenly wanted to talk about kissing Tyler. They were supposed to be clearing the air about

Cassie kissing him. "Wonderful. Amazing. But all I could think about was whether it was as good as when he'd kissed you."

"Oh."

Gemma leaned her head back against the bed's headboard briefly before bringing it up straight again. "How am I supposed to have a relationship with him if I'm constantly thinking about you? No offense."

Cassie smiled a little. "None taken. If it makes you feel any better, that kiss was the most awkward kiss I've ever had."

That was not what Gemma had expected to hear. "Really?"

"Oh my gosh." Cassie made a face. "He cut my lip open with his braces. I sure hope he's learned a little about kissing since then."

If the other night was any indication, he definitely had. Gemma patted her sister's thigh. "Thanks for telling me that, Cass. And thanks for being here. I'm still sorry about your trip."

Cassie waved away her apology. "Don't be. I'm glad I'm here."

"Are you and Drew going to be okay?" Gemma didn't like the hint of sadness that had entered her sister's eyes. It was so different than a couple weeks ago when she'd gushed about a possible engagement.

Cassie looked at her hands for a moment before she spoke. "I don't know. We had a fight a few days before we were supposed to leave for Mexico. That's part of why I came here instead. I need a little time away from him to reevaluate a few things."

"Do you want to talk about it?" Gemma asked. They were never the kind of sisters to talk about boys and relationships before, but maybe it was time to start.

A soft buzz from Cassie's phone prevented her from responding right away. She pulled out her phone, and a small smirk appeared on her face as she read the message and typed out a quick response. What was that about?

"Maybe later," she said after she'd finished. When she looked up, the sadness was gone. "We were talking about Tyler. I don't have any feelings for him by the way. None. I never have. Please don't hold what happened against him. He's a good guy."

The best. So good that not being with him made Gemma's heart literally ache. All these years she'd buried her resentment toward her sister, telling herself that for the sake of their relationship as twins, it was better to blame Tyler. But perhaps at least part of the blame was on her for not coming clean about how she felt in the first place.

And she missed him. The forty-eight hours since she'd seen him were long enough. She slid off the bed and retrieved her phone from the dresser. "Would you excuse me? I have to make a call."

Cassie raised her brows knowingly. "I think you do." She walked to the door. "I really am sorry."

"It's okay," Gemma said. And she meant it. No one could change what had happened, but she felt better after clearing the air.

She found Tyler's number in her contacts and took a deep breath before initiating the call. Her nerves escalated with each ring, and she wondered if he'd pick up. He hadn't even tried to reach out since the game. Was the reason for that because she'd asked him not to? What if he'd stayed away because he was upset about being judged? After all the resistance she'd given him in the last few weeks, was this the final straw?

When his voicemail kicked in, Gemma was about to leave a message when she heard the branches of the oak tree right outside her open window rustle with too much force to be caused by the gentle breeze. She glanced in that direction only to find the branches jerking this way and that like something—or someone—was tugging on them.

Weird.

Even weirder were the deep grunts accompanying the quick jerks of the branches.

Tossing her phone onto the bed, she walked over to investigate. After removing the screen and setting it against the wall, she stuck her head out and looked down.

"Tyler?"

She had a hard time holding back a giggle at the state of him squeezing his adult body through the tight branches as he slowly made his way up to the window. He stopped when he heard his name.

"What are you doing?" she asked, this time with a noticeable wobble of amusement in the words.

"Isn't it obvious?" he asked, reaching for another branch and heaving himself upward with a grunt. "I'm climbing a tree."

"I can see that." Then a thought occurred to her. Hers wasn't the only room along the back of the house. "How did you know this room was mine?"

Tyler paused again. "I realized about halfway up that I didn't, but by then I was already invested."

Gemma raised an eyebrow, and one side of his mouth quirked up.

"Or maybe I texted Cassie and she told me." With one more heave, the top of his head was level with the bottom of the window ledge. He reached a hand up to her. Grabbing it with both of hers, she pulled him up as he pushed himself into the room.

"Why did you climb up the tree?" she asked once he was inside. "There's a perfectly good front door downstairs."

Tyler stopped brushing the few twigs and leaves from his shirt and smiled at her, though it was hesitant, unsure. "I thought I'd recreate the good old days. Like how we used to climb into each other's rooms when we lived next door."

"Correction, *you* always climbed into *my* room." Gemma pointed a finger at him. "Not the other way around."

"Fair enough." He winced. "I'll tell you what, climbing trees was a lot easier when I was a scrawny kid. I think I scratched my back on one of those branches down there. Do you mind checking for blood?"

Before she could respond, he turned around and lifted his shirt, exposing the lean muscles of his back. Gemma sucked in a breath, and not because of the thin red scratch running almost parallel to his spine. It was a few inches in length and ended just above his waistline.

"I think y-you're good," she said, resisting the urge to trace a finger over the mark. Instead, she patted his shoulder twice. "There's a scratch but no blood."

Tyler sighed with relief. "Good. I really like this shirt. It would be a shame to ruin it."

Gemma giggled as he turned around. "Really, Ty. Why didn't you just use the door?"

Tyler's eyes turned uncertain again, and he hesitated before taking a step closer to her. "Because I didn't think you'd answer." He reached out to grab her hands, then stopped and let his arms fall to his sides. "I know you told me you needed space, and I respect that. But I'm asking you to hear me out. Just listen to what I have to say. If, at the end, you decide that I'm nothing but a big jerk and don't want anything to do with me, I'll leave you alone and never bother you again."

"I'm listening."

Tyler's blue eyes searched her face for a moment before he continued. "Gemma, I'm sorry for hurting you. I'm sorry for kissing your sister, but most of all, I'm sorry for not realizing there was something more between us than I was able to see."

He reached for both her hands again, and she found herself stepping a fraction of an inch closer to him, as if an invisible string pulled them together.

"I should've put a stop to the kiss before it started. I don't even know why I didn't," he continued, the pleading in his eyes tugging at Gemma's sympathies. "But Cassie isn't the girl I've wondered about since I moved away. You are. You're the one I've missed every single day for the last seven years. And you're the one I love."

"Love?" Gemma's heart lightened, and she couldn't help when her mouth curved up.

"I may not have realized it back then, but I have no doubt now." He brought both her hands to his lips and pressed a kiss to her fingers. "I know I hurt you in the past, and I am truly, *truly* sorry. If I could go back in time, I'd fix it in a heartbeat. Unfortunately, I can't do that. But I promise to prove to you every day that you're the only one for me. If you'll let me."

She felt the sincerity of his declaration deep in her core. Taking one last step to him, she closed what little space was still between them. "Thank you for apologizing," she whispered, laying her hands flat against his chest. "And for taking my feelings seriously."

Tyler pressed a kiss against her forehead. "I'll always take your feelings seriously. I would've rather had you call me out for my stupidity than hold onto it silently for years." He cradled her head in his hands, lifting her chin to look her in the eyes. "I mean that completely."

Gemma squeezed her eyes closed, feeling the last of her misgivings fade away with his affections. When she opened them again, she held the gaze of the only guy she'd ever truly loved. "I believe you. And you were right. I *was* judging you. But you've been nothing but supportive of me through everything the last two weeks. I'm sorry for not recognizing that sooner."

Tyler's hands slid down her upper arms to wrap around her waist. "What do you say we put this whole thing behind us and start over?"

Gemma looked away briefly before glancing coyly up at him through her lashes. "I *have* loved you since we were ten. I think I can let your little kiss slide this one time."

The upward curve of his mouth was way too tempting for her to resist any longer. Stretching onto her toes again, she gave him a quick peck. Then she pulled back quickly.

"But don't let it happen again," she said, poking him in the sternum.

Tyler took her hands again, tangling their fingers together and bringing them to rest against his chest. "Darling, from now on, the only person these lips will be kissing is you." To prove it, he pressed another long kiss to her forehead, then moved down to kiss the tip of her nose, then both cheeks.

Gemma felt as though she'd melt if he weren't holding her steady. "Darling?" she asked.

He shrugged a shoulder. "You vetoed Slugger, so I had to come up with something else. I can keep thinking if you don't like this one either."

"No, I love it."

He bent his head, his lips brushing hers in a whisper of a kiss before he murmured, "And I love *you*."

He gave her no time to respond before continuing his heartfelt declaration with his lips. This time, Gemma's thoughts stayed firmly in the moment, all the doubts and insecurities put to rest by Tyler's sweet assurances that his heart belonged to her. No matter what happened in the past, it was not her future. He'd more than proved that to her.

The kiss deepened, and she lost herself in his affections, a sweet cocktail of pleasure and adoration. That was exactly how she felt right now. Adored. Treasured. In a way she'd never felt before.

Goose bumps rose on her arms as his hands ran down them until they found her waist, pulling her even closer. Circling her arms around his neck, she felt his heart beating a rapid rhythm against her chest, matching her own until ...

A quick tap on the door preceded its opening. "Gem, do you know where—"

Gemma and Tyler jerked away from each other, the seal of their lips breaking with a smack.

Cassie took one look at them, still locked in an embrace. Her eyes grew wide as they danced between both Tyler and Gemma. "Oh ... uh ... never mind. I'll find it myself." She backed out of the room with exaggerated tiptoes, sending two thumbs up to her sister before slowly closing the door behind her.

Gemma stared at the door for a second, heat traveling up her neck. *Oh, how the tables have turned,* she couldn't help but think. But for the first time, the past didn't hurt. She swiveled her face to meet Tyler's. His guilty expression made her dissolve into laughter. After a few seconds, he joined in, folding her in his arms as they worked to compose themselves at the irony of being caught making out in her bedroom.

She leaned her cheek against his collarbone, more content—no, happy—than she'd been in a long time.

Tyler placed a soft kiss on her hair, then stepped back, keeping his hands cupped gently around her upper arms. "We should probably ..." He flicked his head toward the closed bedroom door. Then he winked.

That wink unleashed Gemma's full smile, and she nodded, even though she'd rather stay here and kiss him a little longer. Then again, there'd be more time for that later.

Slinging his arm over her shoulders, he tucked her in close and they left the room. As she rested her head against his side, she couldn't help but think back to that sixteen-year-old girl crying herself to sleep the night her entire world crumbled on top of her.

Part of her wished she could step into a time machine and go back to visit that girl. She'd give her a big hug and tell her that everything would work out. That she'd get the guy in the end. But more importantly, that she'd be okay.

But she couldn't go back. She could only move forward. Only now, her journey through life would be sweeter with her favorite person by her side.

Epilogue

One Month Later

"I can't believe my first baby is graduating from college today." Mom beamed at Tyler as she reached out to straighten his tie. "I'm so proud of you."

He squirmed a little when she moved on to brush the imaginary wrinkles from his pressed white dress shirt. "Thanks, Mom. I'm glad you're here."

"We wouldn't have missed it for anything," she said, indicating Dad, who was on the other side of the room chatting with Uncle Brent.

Aunt Claire was performing the same maternal grooming habits to Brad a few feet away. "It seems like only yesterday you boys were bugging your younger sisters at family gatherings."

"That's because it *was* yesterday," Beej said, scrunching her nose at her older brother.

"Ha. Funny." Brad flicked a few of her curls into her face as she passed by on her way to the couch. "Admit it, you'll miss me when I move away next month."

"I'll think about it."

She squeezed onto the couch between Kendall and Hallie. The two women moved over to make room, sending a tidal wave of shifting among Elise, Beej's younger sister Brooklyn, and ending with Wes—his shirt already untucked and his tie hanging loose around his neck. He gave up the fight and slid to the floor.

"Are we ready to go?" Dad asked, checking his watch as he crossed the room to stand by his wife. "Parking will be tight near campus today. We don't want to cut it too close."

"We're still waiting for one more person." Tyler glanced out the window, but there was no sign of Gemma. The text she'd sent a few minutes ago said she was leaving. "She should be here soon."

"*She?*" Mom asked, her face lighting up like a kid on Christmas morning. "You mean, we finally get to meet this new girl you're dating? You've been so secretive about her."

He pursed his lips trying to hold back a smile. "I wasn't trying to be secretive. Our relationship is still new. I didn't want to jinx it." That wasn't necessarily true. Now that he and Gemma were together, there was nothing superstitious about their relationship. Even amid the stress of end-of-year assignments, finals, and preparing for a move to Berkeley, the last month with her had been the happiest he could remember ever being in his life. But she'd had such a close relationship with Mom, he knew right from the beginning he wanted to surprise his parents with the happy news.

Dad chuckled. "Your mom even tried to get the girls to spill the deets about her identity."

"Spill the deets?" Elise made a face. "Dad, no one says that." To Tyler, she said, "Don't worry. We didn't tell. Although Hallie did come close the other day. Mom can be very persuasive."

"Never mind that." Mom made a shooing motion with both hands. "Could she be the one? I'm ready for grandkids."

"Mom, it's been a month. Chill." Tyler's smile took the sting out of his words. He wasn't ready to think about making his mother a grandma, but there was no doubt in his mind it would happen someday in the future.

A knock beat Mom to whatever response she was about to make. *Finally!*

"I'll get it. That's probably her." He left the room eagerly, excited to be with Gemma again, even though he'd just seen her last night.

"Hey, graduate," she said once he'd thrown open the door. Her eyes sparkled, the sleeveless blouse she was wearing making them appear more green than hazel. "How do you feel?"

"Relieved actually." He stepped onto the porch and shut the door. The day ahead was going to be a busy one, and he didn't know when they'd have a few minutes alone again.

Her blouse was silky against his palms as he slipped his hands onto her waist, tugging her closer to him, amazed again at how right she felt in his arms like this. Once they'd had all the tough conversations, things had fallen into place so easily. He never realized love could feel like this. Like his life was complete simply because she was in it. If that sounded sappy, he'd gladly roll in it.

Gemma slid her hands up his chest to wrap around his shoulders as he captured her lips in his. For the next few minutes, neither of them spoke, both too distracted by other things.

Finally, she pulled away. "As much as I'd love to stand here kissing you like this"—she gave his lips another peck—"I don't want you to miss your graduation."

"What graduation?" He leaned in for a little more lip action, but Gemma turned her face to the side and all he got was her cheek.

Weaving their fingers together, she stepped back, smirking up at him. "You've worked too hard to pass calculus to miss out on the celebration."

That drew a chuckle from him. "Thanks for helping me study for that final."

"Of course," she said. "Anything to spend time with you. And now you'll never have to take another math class again."

Tyler tilted his head back in relief. "Hallelujah."

The screech of the front window opening broke their attention from each other, and Brad's face appeared through the glass. "Will you two lovebirds stop making out so we can get these introductions over with? At this rate, graduation will be over by the time we even leave the house." He slid the window shut before either Tyler or Gemma could respond.

"We should go in." Tyler placed his hand on the door handle. "I kind of dropped a bomb on my mom when I told her *my girlfriend* was coming and not telling her who you are. My dad is no doubt trying his best to hold her back, but I wouldn't be surprised if she manages to break free soon."

Gemma laughed. "Let's not keep her waiting, then."

He led her inside, situating her behind him so he blocked her from view when they walked into the living room. They had a captivated audience when they entered. "Mom, Dad, I'd like you to meet my girlfriend."

He wished he'd gotten his mother's reaction on camera. When Gemma stepped out from behind him, Mom's hands came up to cover her mouth, and she practically shrieked as she hurried over to them.

"Oh my goodness! Gemma!" Mom threw her arms around Gemma so tightly it was a miracle she didn't knock them both over. "I was hoping it was you."

Tyler did a horrible job at covering up a snort. "What? You didn't even know she was in California."

Keeping one arm around Gemma, Mom reached for him too. He stepped to her, and she brought him into the hug as well. "You're right. I didn't. But I've been hoping for you to end up together since you were kids. And here you are." She pulled back and assessed them both standing next to each other. "First graduation, and now this."

"You're not going to start crying now, are you?" Tyler asked, hoping to get them out the door before the waterworks began.

Mom swatted his arm. "Of course not. If I start now, I'll never stop." She stepped back and clapped her hands together. "Come on, everyone. We better get going. Wes, your shirt is untucked."

"I'll tuck it in when we get there," the youngest Abernathy grumbled, pushing himself off the floor.

Tyler felt Gemma's hand slip into his. He smiled down at her as they joined the throng of people filing out the door. It was almost like old times, how he'd always included her in his family like this. Only it was better now. She was his family. At least, close enough.

For now.

Gemma covered a yawn with her hand and leaned her head against Tyler's shoulder. The gentle rocking of the porch swing lulled her into a state of relaxed contentment as twilight fell around them.

"Are you tired?" His arm, which was draped across the back of the swing, came around her shoulders, tucking her more comfortably at his side.

"A little. Gram had a rough night last night, and it was my turn to help her, so I didn't get as much sleep as I wanted to." Cassie had already gone back to New York, but Mom and Dad both planned to stay through the summer to spend time with Gram and help with her care.

Gram had improved much quicker than even Dr. Fields had expected, but they were still doubtful that she'd be able to return to her former level of health. The next few months would tell what kind of long-term care she would need.

Tyler planted a kiss on top of Gemma's hair. "I'm sure the lack of downtime today hasn't helped."

The day had been nonstop. In a good way. After the graduation ceremony, Gemma accompanied Tyler and his family to a celebration party hosted by the dean of the journalism department before meeting up with the Lucases again for dinner at Trattoria d'Italia in Buena Hills. As exhausting as the day had been, she was amazed at how right it felt to be with the Abernathys again. They were such an important part of her life as a kid that it didn't feel like she'd just spent a first day with her new boyfriend's family.

They already felt like *her* family.

"It was a good day." She turned her head to rest her chin on his shoulder. "And now we have a whole month together before you move up north."

The prospect of a long-distance relationship didn't thrill her, especially with theirs so new, but at least he'd be in the same state.

That was a lot better than the distance between Santiago and Miami. And it would only be for a few years. Their time apart would be a drop in the bucket compared to the seven years they were separated before.

"Will you come visit me?" he asked. He turned his head to look at her, their faces now only inches apart.

She shrugged, pursing her lips to the side. "If I get around to it." He pinched her side, and she jerked away from him with a small squeak. After she'd slid back into his cozy embrace, she said, "You know I'm going to come visit you every chance I get."

"You better." His gaze was both warm and intense. "You have a habit of ghosting me when I move away."

If it weren't for his cheeky grin, Gemma might have thought he was still hung up over what happened between them. She shook her head anyway. "No more ghosting. I promise. Will you come visit me, or are you done with this place?"

"Darling, as long as you're here, I'll never be done with this place."

No, he wouldn't be done with her. She had no doubt about that. And she knew no matter where they ended up, whether it be California or Chile or anywhere in between, they'd always have each other. He was her best friend, her soulmate. Their lives had been inextricably connected from the time they were ten. She'd tried to ignore it, but in the end, theirs was an impossible bond to break. And she'd always be thankful for that.

Gemma kissed his stubbled cheek before resting her head back on his shoulder. Neither of them said much after that. They didn't have to. A lifetime of conversations lay ahead of them. Years of memories waited to be made and cherished. And a future home stood ready to be built.

Together.

This isn't the end of Tyler and Gemma's love story. Get a peek into their happily ever after by signing up for my newsletter and downloading your free bonus epilogue.

https://BookHip.com/WQJHGPB

Keep reading for a sneak peek at Elise's story in Chasing Her Heart.

Chasing HER Heart
A BELFAST HILLS ROMANCE

Last week of January

Don't look like a tourist.

It wasn't the first time Elise Abernathy had reminded herself to play it cool since entering the cab at the airport. Despite repeating the mantra several times in the last twenty minutes, however, a tourist was exactly what she looked like. She sat in the backseat with her face smooshed against the window as the bustling city whizzed past, a dizzying mixture of stone, concrete, and brick.

She couldn't help it. She was finally in the city that had captivated her since that year-long geography project in eighth grade. The European architecture, the ancient stone cathedrals, pubs on every corner, the hustle and bustle of her favorite city.

Dublin.

Excitement bubbled inside her as she anticipated the adventure ahead—so different than other international trips she'd taken with her family as a child. Her first time in Europe held so much possibility. And she was traveling alone. No parental supervision. This time, *she* was the adult. And she was ready to make Dublin her new home. Well, at least for the next four months.

A wide grin spread across her face. Not even the slight mishap at the airport could derail her enthusiasm. So what if the airline lost one of her bags? They had her phone number and promised to call when they found it. She'd get her stuff back. And if not, things could be replaced—her first day in Dublin couldn't.

The soft chuckle from the front seat pulled her from her thoughts. Peeling her eyes from the scene outside, she sat back against the seat and looked ahead.

"Is this your first time in Dublin, then?" Sean, the driver, was a kind man. With wispy white hair peeking out from his frayed brown driving cap, he reminded Elise of her grandfather. He spoke with a thick brogue, a sing-song quality to his words.

"Am I really that obvious?" She asked, already knowing she was definitely *that* obvious.

He responded with another chuckle. "What brings you to the Emerald Isle, then?"

"I'm here for the study abroad program at Trinity College."

Her stomach gave another flutter of excitement as she thought about the day she'd received the letter of acceptance to Trinity's Art History program for spring semester. She'd danced around her home in Buena Hills with reckless abandon, annoying her roommates to no end. It was a good thing they were also related to her—they still loved her despite her quirks.

Sean made a sound of contemplation. "Grand. That's grand. Your parents must be proud of ya, I'm sure."

Elise smiled. "They are." She pushed down a small wave of homesickness, instead focusing on the adventure ahead.

Before long, the scenery changed from the old, brick buildings of the Dublin metropolis to the historic architecture of Trinity College. Sean pulled to a stop in front of a cement building that housed the apartment that would be Elise's home until the end of May.

He jumped out of the vehicle—much too spryly for a man his age —to retrieve her bags.

Elise climbed out of the car and pushed a handful of euros into Sean's hand. "Keep the change."

"Thank you, thank you," he said, pocketing the money. "Take care of yourself, now."

Elise smiled. "Thank you so much."

With a final wave, Sean got in the cab and drove off, leaving her standing outside the building, as jittery as if she'd just downed several cups of straight caffeine. With a centering breath, she grabbed the handles of her well-loved suitcases—the two that had made it into her possession—and walked inside.

She found the office without much problem, though it could be more accurately described as a closet. A single desk and chair fit in the small room with barely enough space for one other person to enter. The door was open, so Elise stepped inside, crowding her suitcases in behind her.

A woman sat behind the desk, typing at an ancient computer. Strands of gray sprinkled her flaming bun of hair. She stared at the screen over square glasses. A small, rectangular, gold plaque that read *Siobhan-Property Manager* sat next to the computer.

Siobhan looked up when Elise entered. "And what can I do for ya?" she asked, taking off her glasses and placing them on her head. She didn't seem unkind, but her piercing green eyes signaled she was not a woman to be crossed.

"Elise Abernathy. I'm here to check in."

"Ah, let me see now." Siobhan placed her glasses back on her nose and consulted the computer, clicking a few times on the mouse and muttering to herself. "Abernathy, Abernathy ... hm ... You don't seem to be in our system." She looked at Elise over the top of her glasses. "Are you sure you have the right address?"

"Yes, I'm positive this is the right place." A small trickle of doubt settled in Elise's stomach.

Siobhan focused on the screen again. "Let's have a look one more time, shall we? Will you spell your surname for me, please? I want to make sure I have it correct."

Elise spelled her last name slowly. Siobhan scrolled through the list before removing her glasses and glancing at her once more.

"I'm sorry, Ms. Abernathy, you are not on the list. I'm afraid there is no flat assignment for you."

"There must be some mistake." Elise's anxiety grew. Here she was in a foreign country by herself, and she had nowhere to stay. "I paid my deposit several weeks ago."

Siobhan pursed her lips. "I'm not sure what to tell you. Do you have a confirmation?"

Now that she thought of it, Elise didn't remember getting an email confirming her deposit went through. In fact, she never even received a room assignment. Figuring she'd get it when she checked in, she hadn't thought much about it. "Not with me, no. Is there any other apartment available? I can pay the deposit right now."

Siobhan shook her head. "I'm sorry. The building is full."

Elise took a deep breath, trying to remain calm, though her forehead pulsed in the beginnings of a stress headache. "There must be something you can do. I *know* I paid the deposit. I should be on the list. Can you please check again?"

Siobhan's expression was full of sympathy. "I'm sorry Ms. Abernathy. There's really nothing I can do if you're not on the list."

Elise's shoulders slumped. For a moment, she stood inside the tiny hole of an office, unable to move. What was she supposed to do now? All she wanted was to get settled in her apartment. And maybe grab a bite. It'd been a while since she'd eaten.

Grabbing the handles of her suitcases, she maneuvered her way out of the office, muttering a word under her breath that would've warranted having her mouth washed out with soap when she was younger. She stepped outside into the chilly winter air, and the cold nipped at her cheeks. At least the sun was out, though it did little to improve her mood. The elation she felt only moments before had left, replaced with the debilitating feeling that she was truly alone.

She grumbled to herself as she trudged down the cobblestone pathway outside the building. First things first, she needed to find a hotel. She'd have to get a room for the night while she figured out what to do. She'd worked her tail off the previous summer and fall, on top of her full class load, often sacrificing her social life so she wouldn't have to worry about money in Ireland. Staying at a hotel for too many nights would eat up her carefully crafted budget. Finding another apartment had to be her number one priority.

Stopping at a bench in a small alcove of trees, their leaves shed for the winter, Elise sat, drawing her coat more closely around her. She pulled her phone from her pocket. Thank goodness she'd set up her cell service before arriving in Ireland. She located a relatively cheap hotel a few blocks away with a vacant room and an early check-in option and booked it before looking up the address in her phone's GPS.

By the time she arrived at the hotel, located above a bar in a quaint but busy tourist area, her shoulders ached from carrying her overstuffed backpack. She found her room, grateful for the small but brightly lit space.

She dropped her backpack on the floor by her bed and collapsed onto the soft, inviting bed. The muted noise of the city hummed in her ear as her eyes fluttered closed, the fatigue finally overcoming her. She'd have to confront her housing situation soon enough, but right now, she needed sleep.

Elise rubbed the sleep from her eyes and looked at the digital clock on the nightstand. The neon red numbers read 13:05. Florida was five hours behind, so it would be eight in the morning back home. Her parents should certainly be up.

Propping a pillow agains the headboard, she pulled herself to a sitting position and grabbed her phone from the bedside table, dialing the landline. She knew from experience that her mom didn't always have her cell with her at this time of day.

"Jason Abernathy." Her father's deep voice was an instant comfort to the unfamiliarity of being in a foreign country by herself.

"Hey, Dad."

"Elise! I've been hoping to hear from you. How was the flight? Are you getting settled?"

Elise picked up the pen on the nightstand and twirled it in her fingers to give her hand something to do. "Actually, I have a bit of a problem. My apartment fell through."

"Oh, that's too bad. Did you pay the deposit?"

She gnawed on her bottom lip with her teeth. "I thought I did. But I don't remember ever receiving a confirmation, so maybe it didn't go through? I don't know. Anyway, I was hoping Mom might know someone over here who could possibly help me find something."

Before her parents married, Mom had been a writer for a travel magazine, often jet-setting to exotic places around the globe and meeting the most fascinating people. Amy Abernathy did not read to her children at bedtime like most parents. Instead, she made up her own elaborate tales inspired by her travels.

Those stories had stirred up big dreams for the wide-eyed little girl in Elise. Even from a young age, she'd made plans to create her own fairytale life of travel. Ireland was only her first stop. Who knew where she'd go from here?

Dad made a noise, bringing her attention back to the conversation. "I'm sure she does. I know she's been to Ireland several times."

"She hasn't left for the café yet, has she?"

"No, she's here. I think she's just getting out of the shower. Let me grab her."

There was a thunk on the line, and Elise pictured her father setting the phone down. He'd probably taken the call at his desk in the home office, where he usually worked in the mornings before leaving for the university. She drummed her fingertips against her cheek as she waited. A moment later, a muffled conversation reached her ears and then Mom's voice came on the line.

"Hey, sweetie. Dad says you're in some trouble."

Elise sighed. "My apartment fell through. I'm in a hotel trying to figure out what to do now."

"Oh, honey. I'm so sorry." Mom clicked her tongue in sympathy. "What a way to start your trip. But I can say that these things happen sometimes. I lost track of how many times plans fell through in my travels. It's something you have to deal with if this is the life you really want."

Elise blew at a strand of straight blonde hair that had escaped her messy top knot and fallen into her face. "I didn't expect everything to go perfect, but I'd hoped that my trip would at least start out smoothly."

Her mom laughed, the light, happy sound bringing a smile to Elise's lips. "Not every day is going to be smooth sailing. The rewards certainly make up for it, though. At least they did in my case. But you should figure out what happened to your deposit. Hopefully, it's only a matter of it not going through and that nothing shady is going on. Whatever the case, I wouldn't wait to figure it out."

"I'll do that," Elise said.

"Tell you what," Mom continued. "I have a friend over there that I've kept in contact with. I used to stay with her and her husband whenever I went to Ireland. She's not in Dublin, but let me give her a call and see if she knows anyone in the area who can help you work out your housing problem."

Relief washed over Elise. She'd landed in Dublin ready to take care of herself and be the adult she was, but sometimes even a twenty-year-old needed her mother. "Thanks, Mom. You're a lifesaver."

"Of course, sweetie. I'm always here for you. I'll call her after we hang up. It might take some time to get a hold of her, though. For now, just stay at the hotel. If it takes a few days to work something out, your father and I will pitch in for the room so you don't have to dip into your savings."

"Okay. Thanks again. I love you."

"I love you too."

Elise hung up feeling slightly better about the situation. Everything would be okay. And after she figured out her housing issue, her time in Dublin would only get better.

Right?

Thank you for reading this sneak peek of Chasing Her Heart. The full novel is available in ebook, Kindle Unlimited, and paperback.

Buena Hills Series

Discovering Her Heart

Book 1

Chasing Her Heart

Book 2

Champion of Her Heart

Book 3

Surrendering His Heart

Book 4

Risking His Heart

Stand-alone Bonus Book

Stay up-to-date on all my new releases by following me on Amazon.

Acknowledgments

After finishing an entire book, you'd think that sitting down to write this section would be a cinch. But how do I adequately thank the many people who had a hand in bringing this story to life?

First of all, I need to thank my amazing friend and critique partner Sarah Madelin for the countless hours you listened to me drone on and on about my anxiety over writing this book. Tyler and Gemma's story wouldn't have come to life without your constant encouragement and support.

To my other two awesome critique partners, Judy Mendelson and Danyelle Ferguson, thank you for your feedback. This book wouldn't be what it is without your suggestions.

It wouldn't be an acknowledgement section without recognizing my incredible editor and cover designer, Raneé S. Clark of Sweetly Us Book Services. As always, thank you for your insights in how to bring out the deeper meaning of this book. You truly understand my vision for this series, and I'm forever grateful for all the hours you've spent on not only this book, but the other two I've written.

Thank you to Kimberly Steinke from Parker Mayne Editorial for helping me put the finishing touches on Tyler and Gemma's story and making it shine. Without you, I still wouldn't know where to put any commas.

Even after publishing three books, my mom, Linda Condie, is still one of my earliest readers. Thank you for constantly supporting me in my dreams. You're the best.

To my husband, David, who patiently allowed me to grill him about his experience growing up as an expat in Thailand, thank you. And thank you for indulging in my fictional world like it's full of real people. I love you!

And to my kids, thank you for being flexible during the times when I needed to work. Part of why I write is to show you that you can accomplish anything you put your mind to, and that hard work pays off. May you always have the courage to chase after your dreams.

Last, but certainly not least, I want to thank you, wonderful reader. There are so many incredible books for you to dive into. Thank you for spending a little time with these characters in Buena Hills. I hope you'll take a chance on future books in the series and beyond.

About the Author

Allison Gygi wrote her first official story in third grade from an old word processor in the computer lab of her elementary school. Since then she has crafted countless tales both on paper and in her head. As a mom, her days are spent trying to find a few minutes to write in between the never ending dishes, meal prep, and helping kids with homework. She loves fairy tales and gravitates towards books with happy endings and swoony kisses. Allison enjoys reading, hiking, and traveling the world. She lives with her husband and three children in a cute suburb of Chicago.

Learn more at https://allisongygi.com

instagram.com/authorallisongygi

amazon.com/stores/Allison-Gygi/author/B0B27C16JN

bookbub.com/profile/allison-gygi